A NET FOR VENUS

A Net for Venus is a study of the heightened emotional relationship between Venetia and her husband Toby which results when she embarks upon a passionate love-affair with Carlo, a young man working in a circus. Exasperation and an increased tenderness alternate in Venetia: jealousy and unselfishness in her husband.

Like many civilized men today, Toby cannot find it in his conscience to blame his wife for her infidelity: his resentment is therefore directed towards his rival, but he faces the dilemma that Carlo is immune from revenge so long as he is necessary to Venetia's happiness and that when her infatuation is over there is no longer any reason for it. Toby's ability to understand his wife's feelings and his attempts to set her happiness before his own open her eyes when contrasted with Carlo's egotism.

This short novel is a more explicit psychological study of human relationships than David Garnett has hitherto written, but in its balance and economy shows the formal perfection and poetic realism which have characterized all his work from *Lady into Fox* to *A Shot in the Dark*.

David Garnett

A NET FOR VENUS ;

394767

LONGMANS

LONGMANS, GREEN AND CO LTD
6 & 7 CLIFFORD STREET, LONDON WI

THIBAULT HOUSE, THIBAULT SQUARE, CAPE TOWN
605–611 LONSDALE STREET, MELBOURNE CI
443 LOCKHART ROAD, HONG KONG
ACCRA, AUCKLAND, IBADAN
KINGSTON (JAMAICA), KUALA LUMPUR
LAHORE, NAIROBI, SALISBURY (RHODESIA)

LONGMANS, GREEN AND CO INC
119 WEST 40TH STREET, NEW YORK 18

LONGMANS, GREEN AND CO
20 CRANFIELD ROAD, TORONTO 16

ORIENT LONGMANS PRIVATE LTD
CALCUTTA, BOMBAY, MADRAS
DELHI, HYDERABAD, DACCA

First Published 1959

PRINTED IN GREAT BRITAIN BY
NORTHUMBERLAND PRESS LIMITED
GATESHEAD ON TYNE

TO

SIGNORA GIOVANNA MADONIA

. . . subtle as spiderwebs, so that not even the blessed Gods could see them, so cunningly were they forged. . . .

ODYSSEY VIII

1

AFTER the circus they paid an extra shilling to join the crowd going to see the ponies in their stables and the animals in their cages. Underfoot was the soiled slippery grass. Where it had broken into slides of mud, sawdust had been thrown in little heaps. The air was full of unfamiliar odours—perhaps of elephants' dung, or tigers' urine—which vaguely thrilled, or alarmed the jostling good-tempered people, pushing and lagging behind, down the roped-off walks in front of the cages. Near to the exit, Toby and Sebastian became aware that Venetia had left them; they had not seen her since they had all been looking at the tigers. The solid mass of fat women, wild children and kindly fathers pushed into them reluctantly, blocked the way and made it impossible to retrieve the missing wife and mother.

Where was she? Why had she disappeared? The big, heavy, limping man waited by the exit, leaning on his rubber-shod stick, his son of sixteen beside him, tall, thin, handsome, frowning angrily, but with a scornful smile coming and going on his full lips. They were unlike: the father with his big head, short iron-grey hair, snub nose and closely clipped

white moustache, had the patient forbearing look of
a friendly seal; the son snuffed the air and spurned
the ground with the proud restlessness of an Arab
pony. At intervals he tossed back his long black hair
and rolled his big, blue, almond-shaped eyes.

The stream of sight-seers, kept in gentle movement
by its own inertia and the cries of the attendants to
'pass along please', reluctantly blundered and pushed
itself out of the animals' quarters and then, breaking up into twos or threes, turned briskly through
the folded back-flaps of canvas into the summer
evening, eager to make for home, tea, and tinned
salmon.

Toby and Sebastian both disliked waiting, but for
different reasons: Toby because standing still soon
became painful, Sebastian because he could not bear
that his mother should make him and his father and
herself conspicuous.

Why did she always lag behind? Or dart across
the street to look at something which she did not
intend to buy in a shop window? Why had she disappeared after the circus? The boy was proud of his
mother's beauty, but to accompany her in a crowded
street was intolerable: men and women turned their
heads to look at her, and such insolence infuriated
him. To go with her shopping was torture for Sebastian. She took ten times as long to buy even the
simplest object as he believed was possible; she made
friends, as though for life, with some degraded

counter-jumper or revolting shopgirl, and as often as not she left behind the purchase she had made, which involved going back to the shop again and listening to her apologies and laughter in another long scene with the debased specimen of humanity who had sold the object to her originally. And here were he and Toby left standing by the exit when the first members of the audience for the second performance could be heard beginning to tramp round the boarded circles of the Big Top, to their seats.

Venetia had suggested their all going to the circus at Reading because it would be a treat for Sebastian, who had returned home from school for a Whitsuntide mid-term holiday. Now, by suddenly disappearing, she was spoiling all his pleasure in the outing. It was typical of their relationship.

'Waiting for Godot,' said Sebastian with what he hoped was bitter irony. He had seen the play and had been bored to tears by it.

Toby laughed. 'Waiting for women can seem almost as boring, but it's more rewarding in the end. Your mother is sure to have had some wonderful adventure which she will describe to us when she turns up.'

But when Venetia did appear and waved to them, she seemed preoccupied, and after telling Toby that he was an owl not to have waited in the car where he could have sat down in comfort and have rested his foot, she fell into a reverie and did not reply to

Sebastian's inquiry as to what on earth she had been doing.

'I know I'm an owl,' said Toby genially, as he drove out of Reading down the Bath Road, 'there's no need to tell me. But I didn't feel sure that you would not hang about near the exit instead of coming to the car.'

'I should have come to the car eventually,' said Venetia, whereupon Sebastian repeated 'eventually!' and uttered a yelp of indignant laughter.

Toby's geniality was not to be diverted, and he began talking enthusiastically about the various acts they had witnessed. He managed indeed to describe the clowns' principal act so well that Venetia began to smile and Sebastian forgot his grievance against her. It was revived, however, a little later, when Toby said:

'The lions and tigers were wonderful. I never expected to enjoy them at all. I felt really envious of their trainer: he was on such good terms with them.'

'I've just been introduced to him,' said Venetia with a touch of *bravura* as she made her confession. 'He took me into one of the cages with a tiger.'

'Good God!' exclaimed Toby, and would have said more had not Sebastian leaned forward from the back seat and shouted at his mother in fury:

'You are the most selfish pig I ever heard of. That is if you are telling the truth,' he added in barely

4

audible tones, but his next remark, 'If you are not, you are just a plain bitch,' was inaudible to his parents.

'I will not allow you to shout things like that at me,' said Venetia in a frozen voice. 'Toby, you must make Sebastian apologize.'

'You called me an owl just now,' said Toby. 'I think we are a whole family of owls and screeching at each other only shows how owlish we are. But I must say I think you are the most enterprising and adventurous mother that any bad-tempered, bad-mannered, jealous schoolboy has ever been lucky enough to have, and for that reason alone, Sebastian, you ought to ask to be forgiven. A pig is the very last creature that Venetia resembles.'

For a few miles they drove in silence. Then when they had left the main road soon after Newbury and had begun to climb the narrow chalk road that led to The Old Forge, Sebastian leaned forward and said:

'I am very sorry that I said that to you. I lost my temper because you made me feel jealous.'

Venetia turned in her seat beside Toby and leaned back and ruffled the boy's hair. Then, while Toby was putting the car away after their arrival and closing the sliding doors of the garage, mother and son embraced. But Sebastian felt that there was something being withheld from him and, as he followed Venetia into the house, his lips curled scornfully and he said to himself:

'But you were rather a bitch to go off and enjoy the tigers all by yourself, leaving Toby and me waiting for twenty minutes when you know it hurts him to stand, and you must have known that I would have given my eyes to go into a tiger's cage.'

Toby was cheerful at supper and opened a bottle of wine.

'Tell us about the tiger,' he said as he filled Venetia's glass.

'There isn't anything to tell, really.'

'I thought tigers were always quite untrustworthy brutes.'

'This one didn't seem to mind me at all.'

'Well, do describe him a bit more.'

'He was magnificent. So was the trainer—you saw him yourself. He talked to the tiger in French and called him "*tu*".'

It was not only the tiger and its trainer of which Venetia was reluctant to speak, but the young man who had unexpectedly invited her to enter the cage and whose handsome face had lit up in astonishment when she had accepted. Something about his dark eyes and cool olive skin had greatly attracted her.

Though Toby was cheerful throughout the meal, Sebastian was morose. He was going back to school next day.

The expedition to the circus had been a failure.

When Toby went up to the bedroom, Venetia was in bed and was already asleep with the reading lamp

6

shining full on her face and the book she had been reading open in her hand. Toby took it from her limp fingers and looked at her. Her long, thin face looked even longer and thinner when her great almond-shaped blue eyes were shut and when her long, blue-black hair hid her ear and rippled down over her shoulder to below her breast. Her full lips were faintly parted, the brown mole on her right cheek gave her beauty, which was grave and Greek, a touch of insolence. She was sound asleep and, as always under all circumstances and all occasions, she was lovely.

Toby undressed quickly, limped into the bathroom next door and, when he came back, unfastened his artificial leg and put it into its box quickly. He was ashamed of his mutilation though he had come by it honourably, and had indeed been given a decoration for his behaviour when he had been wounded. He never allowed Venetia to see his artificial leg if it was possible to keep it out of her sight, and he was always careful not to let the stump four inches below the knee touch her body.

He switched out the light, got into bed and thought about their evening at the circus. Bad luck. No, not bad luck. Inevitable. And the feeling of depression lasted long after he had fallen asleep, and his dreams were of trivial details, each of which had become horribly significant.

Toby Barnard had been a scientist and an aircraft

engineer who had been appointed as consultant and buyer by one of the big Dominion Air Lines. He was not lazy, but he left most of the day-to-day business which this involved to his secretary, Angela Smith, because, after working with him for four years, she had become perfectly competent to do it. For most of the week Angela worked alone in the London office. Then she would come down to the country, and Toby would spend a day or two dictating to her, or if an important visitor arrived in London, Toby would go up to take him out to lunch, or to tour one or two of the aircraft factories. Sometimes, in spite of Venetia's protests, he would bring such a visitor down for the week-end, and on such occasions Angela was always one of the party. She might be wanted to take down the heads of a memorandum or a contract, and she played a good hand at bridge. Thus during the last four years Angela had become almost a part of the Barnard household. Frequently she would confide to one of her intimate friends that she was a fool to go on with the job, and was on the point of giving it up. But then Toby would take her out to the theatre, or to dinner, or would interrupt his dictation to stand up and limp across the room and ruffle her hair, and Angela would feel that for the moment life was worth living again.

Between Venetia and Angela there was an uneasy relationship that two women often show when each of them is aware that the other has qualities complementary to her own. Venetia respected Angela's practical intelligence and her fidelity and devotion to Toby. Angela, on the other hand, often hated Venetia and despised her for what she considered to be her stupidity. She hated her because Toby was in love with her, she hated her for her beauty, and she hated her all the more for never showing the slightest jealousy when Toby took her out, or was particularly nice to her.

It may have shown stupidity in Venetia to be so unaware of Angela's feelings for her, but she was an unsuspicious character. Moreover, Angela did not hate her all the time, but only when Toby allowed his infatuation for his wife to become apparent, or when Venetia was looking more than usually lovely.

It was Sebastian's habit to tot up in his mind the good and the bad in parallel columns and strike a balance between them, thus:

I found a peewit's nest with four eggs.	One of the goldfish is dead and floating upside down in the lily pool.

Slightly down on the morning's walk.

He was especially prone to such forms of calculation at the end of the holidays, and at the end of term. On the morning after the circus, bad clearly predominated. The only major item that he could set against all the bad was the absence of Angela. She, thank goodness, had not been down to The Old Forge at Whitsun. Sebastian detested her. He resented the way in which she ostentatiously and smilingly discounted all his opinions, as though a schoolboy could not be a rational human being. He hated the way in which she doted on his father, and the proprietary manner in which she fussed over him. He had discovered her dislike of his mother. In his opinion Angela was a schemer, and he could not make out how Toby could put up with her, and what enabled Venetia to turn a blind eye.

With Angela absent everything ought to have been perfect, but in fact there had been something wrong. At Christmas Venetia had been riotous: dressing up, dancing and singing about the house, and continually playing jokes on him and Toby. But, all through the Easter holidays, she had been wrapped up in herself and off-hand in her manner. Several times she had snubbed him, or had snapped at Toby. And now at Whitsun she was even worse. What Sebastian minded most was that she had made wounding or disobliging remarks about the house and its neighbourhood. Sebastian worshipped The Old Forge. The house had, as its name implied, been converted from a smithy and two adjacent cottages, while what was now the big drawing-room, where the Barnards occasionally gave parties, had once been a wheelwright's shop.

The resulting mass of buildings was a typically twentieth-century, upper-class English country dwelling. On the ground floor was a hotchpotch of little rooms on different levels, leading out of a big irregular hall into which a big modern oak staircase descended, though all round were ancient fifteenth-century beams and ingle nooks. Upstairs Venetia and Toby shared a big bedroom; the others were tucked away at the ends of long, winding passages, with steps up and steps down. There was a lovely view of the downs out of some of the windows. Although the atmosphere was intentionally old-world, everything had been made extremely comfortable, with central heating and electric fires, and thick carpets and Jacobean gate-legged tables everywhere, and a row of detective stories in each of the spare rooms. Everything was tidily in its place, with well-dusted china dogs on the mantelpieces and polished brass trays in the hall. There was quite a number of good books in the house, but none of the pictures was worth attention.

Outside, the low buildings, partly brick and tile, partly cob and thatch, were buried in a big garden which nestled under the chalk down. There was a big box tree, an ancient yew and a younger copper beech. Between a wealth of flower-beds, the lawn ran back to the summer-house and the swimming-pool in which, during summer, Sebastian and Venetia took morning and afternoon bathes. Sebastian loved every square yard, but on Sunday morning Venetia had said:

'We can't help getting mouldier and mouldier if we go on living in a place like this.' It was sheer blasphemy, and Sebastian could only hope that it was intended as such.

The same day Venetia had wantonly told Toby that she was tired of seeing the three silver cups, which he had won years ago sculling, on the side-board in the hall.

'Can't you hide them away somewhere else?'

His father had agreed to put them in his study, and his mother had continued in the most bloody-minded way:

'You might get rid of that pair of sculls in the big room at the same time.'

Toby had replied: 'Well, if I must . . .' and Sebastian had told her that she ought to be jolly proud of them, and that she was an unimaginative pig . . . for which he had later apologized. Then there was the scene after the circus last night. It seemed to Sebastian all of a piece: his mother had done a lot to spoil the Easter holidays, though the weather and the absence of rabbits owing to myxom-atosis had helped—not that shooting was possible at

Easter. And then she had done the same at Whit-sun. It was a gloomy, grown-up Sebastian who returned to school. Venetia, who had felt his censori-ousness, but who could not shake off her mood, was not altogether sorry to see him go.

2

VENETIA had given exhibition dances when she was in an E.N.S.A. company during the war, but she had danced little since Toby had been invalided out of the R.A.F. However she danced whenever she could, and Toby was not surprised when, ten days after the visit to the circus, she told him that she had accepted an invitation to a dance.

'I said I thought you wouldn't be able to come as you had to be in London on business that night. It's Lady Ida Benskin, and it's a party as well as a dance.'

Lady Ida had a reputation for eccentricity and for giving quite unusual parties—at which anything might happen and at which one was sure to meet new people. Her parties were a feature of Wiltshire country life, and were discussed for months after they had taken place. Many of the guests laughed at their hostess, but her invitations were sought after. Toby and Venetia had not received one before because she lived right on the other side of the county. Recollecting all this Toby said: 'Oh, I'll come. I expect I shall enjoy it. I'm sure there will be lots of pretty girls who don't dance and will be delighted to sit out with me.'

There were as many as Toby could have hoped for, and in other ways Lady Ida proved to have a *flair* for inviting strange mixtures of people and offering them the right kind of food and drink.

Toby and Venetia were soon separated. He found himself among some old friends, and was then carried off to take a French film star in to supper. Venetia he saw defending herself so eagerly, and then counter-attacking her *vis-à-vis* with such grace, that the word *sparkler* came into his mind, and he missed a whole sentence from his lovely companion as the thought of Venetia as a small child holding a sparkler firework in its hand, and whirling it in all directions, came to amuse him.

When Toby listened again the French girl was saying: 'Tell me, is our hostess a respectable woman? She behaved with that young man opposite as though she wanted to—how do you say *afficher*?'

'Publish,' prompted Toby.

'. . . then to publish that he was her lover, and she insisted on introducing him to me—and I find—you understand, that he is quite impossible.'

'My wife seems to be enjoying his conversation,' said Toby. 'And I can assure you that Lady Ida has never been the subject of a breath of scandal.'

The French film actress said no more.

Though the conversation was not so sparkling as Venetia's smile and eyes, it would have surprised Toby had he heard it.

Venetia had instantly recognized the dark eyes and olive skin which looked so smooth, so cool and so inviting.

'Do you remember coming up to me and asking if I would like a better look at one of the tigers?' she asked as she seated herself, turning to her neighbour on the right.

'I've laid awake, thinking about you every night. You are the only one . . .'

'I've lain awake too, thinking about that lovely tiger. I shall never, never forget stroking his furry ears. What an extraordinary chance we should find ourselves here, sitting side by side. I couldn't believe my eyes when I saw you.'

'I certainly don't belong in this outfit. I'm not a *habitué* of the Lady Ida's. But it's not chance that we met here. It's kismet.'

'Well, you might call it that. I accepted the invitation because I have a passion for dancing and seldom get the chance.'

'Care to dance with me after supper? I'm crazy on it.'

'Do you dance the tango?'

'Do I not? Tango's my middle name. Honestly this is kismet,' and Carlo pressed her knee with his own.

Venetia laughed with slight embarrassment, and her neighbour immediately changed his tone, as he asked:

'You don't believe in fate?'

'No, I believe in tigers.' And turning to her neighbour on the left Venetia asked:

'Do you know if there is a god or goddess of the tigers in India?'

Old Josiah Fancourt thought that there were only local deities.

'Of course, my dear lady, I speak subject to correction. But I believe Buddha was a tiger in one of his incarnations and his wife was a tigress.'

'What a happy marriage that must have been,' said Venetia with conviction. It seemed to her that tigers must be happier together than human beings could be.

After supper there was dancing, and the French actress, having been claimed by a partner, Toby went to gossip with some non-dancers. But then, hearing some applause and divining who had aroused it, he limped to the edge of the ball-room to look on. The floor was empty except for Venetia and a dark young man who were dancing the tango. Venetia had been a brilliant dancer when Toby married her, but he was astonished by the perfection with which she was dancing. Her partner, who looked as though he might be Spanish, was obviously a professional. They were perfectly matched; the dance was a unity; their two bodies the complement of one directing passion. Toby, who had been a good dancer himself, was delighted.

There was more applause in which Toby joined, and then Lady Ida announced that there was to be an interval: would everyone fill his and his partner's glass with champagne and listen to a story that Carlo was going to tell them? As it was going to be rather a long story, it would be a good plan to have a bottle of champagne at hand for those who might get thirsty while listening to it.

A chair was put in the centre of the floor: there was a popping of corks, girls subsided gracefully round the edges of the room and Venetia's young partner walked out into the middle of the ball-room. A light lit up his face and the rest of the room was switched into semi-darkness. Carlo sat down, leaned forward and began to speak with extreme confidence in an unpleasant voice, with the worst sort of semi-cultured, Cockney accent.

But, after the first sentence, the voice and accent were overlooked because of the eagerness and vitality he showed in telling his story. It was obviously alive to him as he told it and somehow he imparted the vivid pleasure he took in recalling it.

'I belong to the circus. I wasn't born to it like many performers. Well, this is a story of the time when I joined. Not the circus I'm in now but a smaller one. The man who seemed to boss the whole show was a midget: a Sicilian called Nenni. He wasn't like the majority of midgets, because he was very nearly to scale: a well-shaped man, but only three foot four inches in height. He was the most conceited man I've ever known. He never spoke much and I shouldn't have got wise to how vain he was if it hadn't been for Roger Poulenc, our Belgian lion-tamer. That man is a hundred per cent. He's the type that would do anything for a joke. Nenni would never pay his share, if he could dodge it—but he never refused anything that was going free. But he could not hold liquor, on account of his size. He'd get high on one whisky, and then, didn't he start talking big! Poulenc got a lot of fun out of getting Nenni oiled up. It didn't set him back a lot standing treat to that little fellow. I was a new boy—had just been taken on for a dance-act with the clown on roller skates, and to help Poulenc with his lions, and I was a bit nervous when I went into the saloon bar on Sunday night where Poulenc was throwing a little party. The set-up was like this: Poulenc is a big fellow, built like a heavy-weight: blond hair and blue eyes. He looks tough on account of being scarred, but he wouldn't hurt a fly except for fun. Well, he was in one corner by the bar. In a row on a sofa were three of our clowns. The fill-in clowns are a lot of has-beens: circus riders or trapezists that have had too many falls, or got too old: mostly bald as coots, bad breath, spend all day talking shop, or yarning about the old days. All the fill-in clowns I've ever met are the same. Then there were three welter-weight Danish girls, and the husband of one of them, and a Mexican equestrienne. I call her that, but she was half-Hindu. She used to send me for the first weeks until I found out how dumb she was. All of them, except Nenni and Poulenc, were really good-tempered types that liked getting together and being cosy after the day's work—they liked a couple of pints of mild and bitter, and a quiet talk about their own prospects for an hour before bed. But walking up and down, bossing them and stopping them being cosy, was little Nenni, his eyes like black olives, his hook nose, his tight little mouth just registered contempt.

'There was something funny between him and Poulenc: I don't mean anything queer, but sort of funny. Nenni wanted to come it over him and make him pay in any way he could. All Poulenc wanted was to get an evening's fun out of Nenni, and the little chap wouldn't stand for it. But he couldn't walk out because he knew there was a free whisky coming. Poulenc had just bought him one when I came in. When Nenni had got down half a glass he started smiling, and was that smile revolting! When the glass was empty he started to orate. I didn't quite get all he said, because his Sicilian accent was new to me then, and he always used the Italian word if it resembled an English one. What I missed that time, I got the chance of learning by heart later on. I used to be nearly word perfect on Nenni's oration, but I have forgotten some bits. It ran like this:

'"I am intelligente. I am the scienza genio. Baird, Marconi, Edison—three ignorant bambini. My machina more wonderful. I will not spik of it to you buffoni. I am artist greater as Cellini: filosofo greater as Einstein. Cellini, Einstein, they are my equals. No others. Not Buonarotti . . . not Da Vinci. Where is my discovery? Secreto. You buffoni can divine never. Never. All here." And Nenni tapped an inch and three-eights forehead with a two-inch forefinger.

'"Poems greater as Dante, as Leopardi! I 'ave them all 'ere." Tap, tap on his teeny brain-box.

'"All 'ere and all secreto. I could vend what I 'ave 'ere for fortune: be millionaire. The rich man of the world. But I will not break my promesso; never to 'elp the 'umanity. I spit on the 'umanity. I will not make the world grander, richer, 'appier for you animali."

'When he said this Nenni looked round at each of us in turn and spat on the floor. He wanted to make it as personal and offensive as he knew how. The Danish girls goggled at him but the clowns didn't even give him a dekko. Poulenc just lapped it up and loved it. Then he bought Nenni another Irish whisky. The midget took a wet and went on:

'"Among the 'umanity I am 'appy to be a freak. A freak with the cervello of Einstein and the—'ow you say—the coleoni of Casanova. There this freak is more than a man. Because of my conformation no woman can resist me. But my 'sdegno for the women is grander to my detestation of the men. I never take a woman for satisfaction, but to dimostrare the 'sdegno I 'ave for 'er 'usband."

'Poulenc was grinning with pure joy: he was getting value for money, but the second John Jameson was more than the little man could take, and he fell over on the floor. Poulenc picked him up like a kid, carried him off and put him to bed. Then I spotted that only Poulenc and I had been listening. The three clowns were still trading gimmicks, and my Mexican Hindu girl-friend was recommending a lodging-house in Blackpool where she had gone for a holiday. Nenni's boasting when he was high with whisky fascinated Poulenc, and it wasn't long before he organized another little party in the saloon bar and got the midget to say his piece. But this time he had borrowed, or hired, a tape recorder which he hid behind the curtains. Next morning he asked me over to his caravan, and we played Nenni's piece over. After that I set myself to learn it.

'Life in a circus has a heap of charm but no privacy, so word of Nenni's recording soon got around. Poulenc had to play it over and over, and we were half-way through one afternoon when I spotted Nenni standing by the steps of the van. The little man's face was terrifying: cobras had nothing on him. I have never seen anything so venomous. But he said nothing: just stood there. When the

23

record finished, I tried to point him out to Poulenc, but the little man had faded out. After that, Nenni would never speak to either of us again, and he had no more use for free whisky. Poulenc had to find his evening fun somewhere else—but, of course, he had the recording—the only catch was that he'd had to return the machine.

'Nenni kept away, and we had forgotten about him when we opened at Bristol, about three months later. Poulenc's act had just been hotted up with a young Bengal tigress called Kali—a lovely thing—but not too trustworthy, as she hadn't settled down in her new home. I was a bit windy of her.

'Poulenc used to have her sent down the tunnel into the cage before any of the others. He wanted to get her on her stand, and keep her there. At the first evening performance, she stopped when she got to the mouth of the tunnel and picked something up just where the bright lights threw a shadow from the door. The other animals were coming down on top of her, and she swung round and hit at the first of them—an old lion called Jupiter. The next moment she went haywire. She let out a roar of pain and thrashed round and round the big cage, and I saw her tear at her lips with her front paws.

'Poulenc was the tops. He only gave one dekko at Kali: then he blocked the mouth of the tunnel and held up the big cats coming down it. Some of

24

them turned, some wouldn't, some couldn't. We had to work them back, prodding at them.

'By that time Poulenc was out of the big cage, and when he had got what he wanted, he went back into it where Kali was throwing herself about and rolling around. Poulenc had made a spring purse net—nylon—that he could shoot. It was his own gen: he got the idea from the pilot parachute that opens the big one. Well he shot his net over Kali and in ten seconds she was all balled up. We rushed in, roped her, lifted her on to a barrow and ran her back for the vet to handle.

'He gave her an intravenous injection of pentethal: not easy. You try shoving a needle into a vein of your house cat. That put her out at once, and he was able to swab out her mouth and wash out her stomach.

'Meanwhile Poulenc was back in the Big Top. I wish I had been there to see, because he put on a wonderful act. The audience was yelling: about a third of them booing and the rest shouting at the others to shut up. Poulenc had all the lights out, except for a spotlight on him. He stood there and covered his face with his hands, his head bent and his big bare shoulders working: he made them all think he was in tears and so they shut up. Then his voice came over the mike, and he gave them the works: Some damned bloody swine had tried to poison his tigress and to murder him: everyone could see what pain she had been suffering. Then he explained that the vet had given her an anaesthetic and was working to save her life. And meanwhile the show would go on without Kali.

'Animal trainers have an awful time with cranks. A lot of these "animal lovers" give themselves a tremendous kick talking about torturing tigers with red-hot bars—but I've never seen anything used except raw meat and the voice, and the whip when he wanted them to snarl.

'Then the lights were turned up, and the lions and tigers came down the tunnel again. Poulenc worked them that time without a whip. He took a chance that day—just fussing them; he put his hands on them, played with their ears and last of all lay down in between the paws of Sara, the old lioness. They didn't do all their tricks, but he did show the crowd that he and his cats were one big family. It was a risk, because without his whip he was at their mercy and they knew it. There were two there which were funny-tempered—but he always kept close to one of the three that he knew would protect him, if either of the others sprang at him. And did the show go over! The audience was clapping and shouting all the time the big cage was being taken down.

'The bit of meat that Kali had picked up was salted with a paste of cayenne pepper.

'It was our Sicilian genius, Nenni, who had tried to get Poulenc killed. The ringmaster seized the little chap's kit and found a few grains of cayenne on the sleeve of his coat: afterwards we found out he had got a half-pound of cayenne from Brooks's in Maiden Lane, a week after he had heard the recording.

'So the boss sacked him.

'Nenni bought it only about a month later in the other circus where he had got himself a job. There was an inquest and the coroner's jury brought in accidental death—but some of us aren't so sure that he wasn't bumped off. At all events Poulenc had no hand in it.

'After Nenni's death, I went round to the rival show and asked—out of mere curiosity—if the midget had left any papers, and this is what the manager told me:

'Yes. There was a little book full of poetry in Italian, written in such a tiny hand that you could scarcely read it without a magnifying glass—also a few blueprints and what looked like mathematical calculations and machine specifications. He didn't know what to do with them, so he had just sent them off to the Podesta of Catania in Sicily—the town where Nenni was born.

'If I ever go to Sicily, I shall try to find out whether they are still in existence.'

Carlo stopped abruptly. 'Thank you, thank you,' came one or two voices. Other guests turned to each other and raised their eyebrows. Not everyone had appreciated the entertainment. Lady Ida turned on the lights and offered Carlo a glass of champagne, and the music began again. Venetia had three more dances with him. After the last dance he took out a pocket comb and ran it through his glossy curls. Venetia was annoyed with herself for feeling a moment's disgust at his doing this. And when he turned and said in a studied offhand manner: 'Care to sit this one out?' she accepted with added warmth.

'Where did you learn?' Carlo asked soon after they had got settled into a dark alcove in the library.

'Learn what? . . . Oh, you mean dancing? I did exhibition dancing with an E.N.S.A. company during the war . . .' And noticing a surprised look on the young man's face, she explained, 'I'm heaps older than you are. I married Toby—my husband—at the beginning of the war when I was only nineteen. He was in the R.A.F., in Coastal Command. I left our baby with my mother-in-law, and went out with an E.N.S.A. company to Egypt and North Africa, and did exhibition dances for three years, until Toby was wounded and grounded. He was Captain of a Sunderland flying-boat and got his foot badly shot up, but he got back and had to have it amputated. Of course I left E.N.S.A. then, and I haven't done much dancing for the last twelve years.'

'Honestly you're a hundred per cent. You're the best partner I ever had. You are marvellous.

Couldn't you date me and have a whole evening dancing?'

Venetia looked at his eager handsome face and found herself saying: 'There's nothing I should like better if it could be arranged.'

'My worry is that the circus moves to Swindon to-morrow, and shall I be busy the whole of next week! But couldn't we meet in Swindon, Tuesday after next?'

'I suppose I might . . . if I can get away.'

'There's a dance hall with a good band, really hot for a town that size.'

'It would be most awful fun,' said Venetia.

They talked for another ten minutes, and then she saw that the room was empty.

'I say, I think everybody's going, or gone.'

Seeing that they were alone together, Carlo put his arms round her and kissed her on the mouth. Venetia laughed and kissed him back, and then, feeling herself beginning to go limp in his arms, she disengaged herself and laughed again.

'That's a promise then?' asked Carlo.

Venetia nodded.

'Suppose I wait here a minute, while you leave. It might give your husband ideas if he saw us come into the room together.'

Venetia laughed. 'It will save me from getting into Lady Ida's bad books for monopolizing you. *Au revoir.*'

'See you later, alligator,' said Carlo.

Venetia laughed, but did not make the reply which was fashionable at the moment.

When she went alone into the ball-room, Toby was sitting drinking and talking to his host. Venetia went across to them and said: 'I suppose we really must go—though I don't want to a bit.'

'We're among the last,' said Toby. They said good-bye, Toby found his stick and coat and limped a little unsteadily after Venetia to where she had parked the little two-seater Triumph which was her own car. They were silent as she drove back along the empty straight road at high speed. Toby said nothing as he watched the needle of the speedometer creep down past eighty, but Venetia must have felt aware of his criticism, for she suddenly asked in a sharp voice: 'What is it?'

'I was only thinking there was no need to die young,' said Toby.

'We aren't young any more,' said Venetia. 'You are nearly fifty and I am thirty-seven, a middle-aged woman. But was I driving too fast for you?'

'Yes. Nearly ninety. I keep wondering what happens if the lights fail at that speed, or if you hit a brick. And I've seen such a lot of people killed who I wish were alive now.'

'I'm sorry. I am tired, and wanted to get home quickly.'

Venetia dropped the speed to a mere fifty-five, but they scarcely spoke again until the next morning, when she turned over in bed and gave Toby an entirely unexpected and very passionate kiss. They had a late breakfast.

3

FOR the first time for so long that she could not remember how long it was, Venetia felt herself tingling with anticipation. Life which went by so rapidly, leaving behind so few and such petty, boring memories, had suddenly slowed up to walking pace: every moment of it precious and intolerable, filled with secret hopes and fears. She had promised Carlo that she would meet him at Swindon, in a fortnight's time. Why had she promised? The certainty that he would make love to her, the possibility that she would take him as her lover, enriched her body and made her skin glow and feel as smooth as if she had been bathing in soft river water, but yet the certainty and the possibility was never dwelt on, or quite admitted to herself.

'Am I in love? Have I fallen in love? Can this wonderful thing have happened to me? I have had no hope of it—seeing so few people and such dull ones.'

The days which divided her from Swindon crawled slowly by, but she made no preparations for her visit and had said nothing to Toby.

Meanwhile, early in July, Angela, a tall girl

with a wide mouth, astonished eyes and a skin like a plum, had arrived for a stay of several days of hard work. Her face had been compared to Hogarth's *Shrimp Girl* by her admirers, and she made the most of her looks by piquant mannerisms: putting her finger in her mouth to show mock coyness, hugging herself in a way which made her pointed breasts more prominent, or listening with her hands pressed together in an attitude of prayer. These little graces amused Toby and Venetia, but they exasperated Sebastian.

Angela's arrival at The Old Forge was always an event. She brought with her an immense amount of detailed work to be dealt with by Toby, so that it was principally at meals, in Venetia's presence, that she blossomed socially, eager to tell stories of what she had been doing in London. She was popular with men, so that there was always a list of the plays to which she had been taken and the parties she had attended, and of the hangovers and misadventures which had resulted. A stranger, listening to these recitals, might have fallen into the error of assuming that Angela was a 'good time girl'. It would, indeed, have surprised some of her male friends if they had known that she was a virgin—for she refused their advances with expert good nature, usually explaining that she could only feel in that way about one person in the world. Father Athelstan greatly enjoyed her confidences, for she was a devout Anglo-Catholic.

Angela had kept a typical adventure to recount at dinner.

'I felt most awfully mean and horribly to blame, for the poor boy had booked a room for us both at Maidenhead for the three days of his leave—at a vast expense I've no doubt. I only discovered that he was in deadly earnest when we were leaving the party. So, as a compromise, I took him on to the Marengo Club where, with my encouragement, he drowned his sorrow so effectively that I had him on my hands and had to take him back to my flat for the night to sober up. Next time I shall stick to my principle that there's safety in numbers.'

Venetia had listened to any number of anecdotes of this sort, and always marvelled at Angela's capacity to avoid what seemed to her the inevitable and desirable conclusion to such adventures. But that evening she did not pay much attention, and when the story seemed to be over, she said:

'By the way, did I tell you, Toby, that I am going to London for the night on Friday?'

'Why?' asked Toby. Venetia said nothing. She was unprepared for the question. Telling the lie had been difficult: to elaborate it would be horrible. Yet the silence, prolonging itself in front of Angela, was unbearable. Toby allowed it to last until Venetia was in misery, then he filled it easily, passing it over as though there had been no moment with an abyss opening between them. Two hours later, when he and Venetia were alone in their bedroom, he returned to the subject.

'It's rather awkward your going off and leaving me alone in the house with Angela,' he said.

'Don't be ridiculous.'

'Well, I don't think Angela will like it.'

'You mean just the opposite. You don't like being left alone with her.'

'Well, I don't really.'

'You'll have to protect yourself as best you can. You are quite experienced and wily enough not to need me as a chaperone. You are just being silly.'

'Why are you staying the night in London?' he asked.

'I've got more to do than I can manage in one day. Besides, I'm driving,' she added, for they usually took the train from Newbury. Toby was unsatisfied, but he asked no more questions. What could she have said? How could she answer him? For she both knew and did not know the answer. Love is a secret, and in spite of the ferment within her she did not know what she would do, or exactly why she was going to Swindon—except that it was to keep a silly promise.

On Friday morning she was escaping from the house when Toby waylaid her.

'When will you be back?' he asked.

'Does it matter so especially? It is difficult to be

sure when one's driving,' Venetia answered. She had been surprised by the note of anger in her first words, and added the explanation in order to try to produce an air of reasonableness.

'Don't drive too fast. I get anxious when you're away.'

Venetia shivered as she drove out on to the main road, as though she were physically shaking off the touch of anxious, loving, possessive hands. Was the whole of her life, and all human relationships in it, to be an endless repetition of the years of subjection to anxious, possessive, parental love? Must she always belong to someone who expected love, as she had belonged, during the first nineteen years of her life, to her mother? Then it had been out of the maternal frying-pan into the fire of Toby's love . . . and then back again into the frying-pan of Sebastian's expectations. These thoughts were blown away as the tiny car tore down the straight stretches of road, hovered at the corners and darted on. She would be at Swindon before the time appointed. But when she walked into the saloon bar of the White Horse, she saw Carlo already waiting, at the rendezvous he had suggested. For the first moment, the difference between the image she had been forming of him and the reality alarmed her. He was not so big as she remembered; beside Toby he would have looked a small man. Also he was shy and consequently brusque.

37

'Good of you to be on the dot. I hate waiting, don't you?'

'I'm a bit early. But I've been longing for you to show me round the circus again.'

'I planned that for the afternoon.'

For a little while, they talked about the circus, then Venetia said: 'As it's a fine day, I thought we might have a picnic. I've brought everything. I thought we could drive to the top of the Downs.'

Carlo's reaction to her car was disagreeable to her.

'You can rely on that for performance! Just what I've always planned to get for myself when I strike lucky in the Pools.'

They got in and she drove slowly out of Swindon past Coate. To stop Carlo talking about cars, she began telling him about Richard Jefferies and the part Coate Reservoir played in his life and in his books, *Bevis* and *After London*. Almost to her surprise, for she was already near to disillusion, Carlo instantly grasped the idea underlying *After London*, was delighted by it, and began inventing touches of his own to make the changes which would be needed to bring a deserted England up to date. They had found a subject which brought them into touch again. The shame of desire without sympathy vanished. Presently she told Carlo that she would lend him the books, remembering, as she said so, that they would be Sebastian's copies.

She drove up on to the high Downs and then off

the road, along a grass track between beeches. Carlo had not touched her, but when she stopped the car and looked at him, he took her face in his hands and kissed her and his tongue probed between her lips.

'Couldn't have waited much longer,' he said.

Venetia made him wait until they had eaten the cold chicken and salad and had drunk the bottle of Côte de Rhone which she provided. Half the bottle seemed to make him a little tipsy. The sun was hot: there were grasshoppers stridulating, and the simplicity of Carlo's love and his appreciation of her beauty and his surprise that she should want him, combined to amuse and charm her, and to fill her with contentment.

The sun warmed her. Mingled with her physical satisfaction was an awareness that she had done a good action: that she had given even more than she had received, and that the hour of love upon the open downland would not quickly be forgotten by him.

For half an hour Carlo slept in her arms, while she looked at him. How simple and easy her life would be if she had courage . . . if Toby . . . Carlo was happy . . . she had found what she needed. When he woke, Carlo was upset and afraid that she had made him late for the afternoon performance. She drove him back like a racing driver. Then she booked a room in the name of Mr. and Mrs. Barnard in a hotel, and left her bag there.

She went off by herself swimming in Coate Reservoir until it was time for the second performance of the circus, then bought herself a ticket, and watched it. When it was over, they left the circus separately, and, without even glancing at the tigers, met at the dance hall. It was half full, with young soldiers, airmen and Teddy boys with shopgirls, and the standard of dancing was low. Venetia and Carlo began to dance, and except for two breaks, when they went out for sandwiches and a drink, they danced together continuously until a little before closing time. As always happens when there are good dancers on the floor, the band rose to the occasion and gave its best. At one moment Carlo would be gentle and stately, in the next dance he would be daemonic and abandoned, and Venetia responded perfectly to his changing mood. Towards the end of the evening, the M.C. came up and asked if they would be willing to do an exhibition dance. They were wildly applauded by the crowd, which at the beginning of the evening had watched them with hostile eyes.

As they walked back to the hotel, they felt that they understood one another perfectly, though they had scarcely spoken all the evening. In spite of a day filled with driving, making love, swimming, going to the circus and dancing for hours on end, Venetia felt not the slightest fatigue as she took Carlo into her arms for the second time, and it was far into the night when they fell asleep.

Next morning they lay for a long time in bed with the windows open, and the early summer sunshine streaming into the room. Carlo began talking about his ambitions: success was what mattered in life, and it did not matter what kind you achieved, for any big success brought the other kinds along with it, if you wanted them.

'If you have the right gimmick, you make a big name. If you get a big name, you get in the big money. If you get in the big money without a name, you can buy yourself one overnight. It doesn't matter which way round it comes. And the sure way to get there is always to be one jump ahead of the other fellow. I learned a lot from watching Poulenc with his big cats. He fixes them so he knows what they are going to do before they know themselves. Men are just the same—and you have to treat them just the same way. I'm crazy about the animals—no one more. But, you know, men and women are really more fun to watch than ponies, or elephants, or those damned cats.'

Venetia remembered what Toby had once told her about Behaviourism, and it seemed to her that Carlo was on the point of arriving independently at the same standpoint. That was creditable surely. But, above all, she was delighted by his eager, simple, unconscious egotism. He was clean and young and filled with an unbounded interest in himself, and she lay smiling, silently watching him, as he artlessly put forward his discoveries. Eventually he must have seen her smile and slightly misinterpreted it, for he said apologetically:

'You must be asking what's bitten me. But you make me feel funny: you make me want to talk to you like we were not in bed, like I've never talked to a woman before. I guess you're my kismet. You'll bring me all the other kinds of success I could want. You know every damned thing though you don't let out a squeak. I didn't know there was two kinds of women before I met you. You're one sort, and the rest is the other.'

Carlo was anxious to avoid being seen with Venetia by the other employees in the circus, who would know that he had not slept in his caravan. 'Those clowns are so prissy they'd get me the sack if they knew about you,' he said. So Venetia drove him to Bath, where they had lunch and at last found a place where they could dance during the afternoon. Then she drove back, dropping him at Swindon. On parting she promised to spend another two days and a night with him when the circus had moved to Bristol the following week.

She got back to The Old Forge in time to change her dress before dinner, but was so tired she could hardly get out of the hot bath. The prospect of having to tell lies in front of Angela, in reply to Toby's questions was scarcely to be faced. She felt sure she would break down. However, no questions were asked, Angela was unusually subdued and the meal passed off flatly enough. The only lie that Venetia told was the quite unnecessary one that she was sorry to be so glum, but that she had toothache. On hearing this, Toby insisted on her taking a tablet of codeine and a glass of brandy and sent her off to bed with a hot-water bottle, although it was the middle of summer. When Toby came to bed, she turned towards him and opened her arms. She felt that she could not bear to lie in the same bed with him restless and unhappy. If she could not give him love, she could give him something very like it.

Two days later, she complained again of toothache and said she would make an appointment with her dentist and go up to London for the night on the following week. Toby, though he knew nothing, seemed filled with anxiety and Angela, who was staying for several days to finish a long report on a new turbo-jet engine, seemed to Venetia to avoid being left alone with her. There was an odd uneasiness between the three of them at meals.

When Angela was at The Old Forge, she sometimes filled up her spare time by washing and polishing Toby's ancient Lanchester. The day after Venetia's return she did the same for the little two-seater Triumph and, while brushing it out, picked up two counterfoils with the printed words: *Swindon Palais de Dance. No Readmission. Gala Night 6th July.* It was the date of Venetia's unexplained visit to London. How could she have gone via Swindon, thirty miles in the opposite direction? It was impossible. She must have gone to Swindon instead of to London, and have only spoken of London to conceal where she was going. The discovery filled Angela with a wave of cold anger, for to deceive Toby seemed to her to be unforgivably base. This was followed by a thrill of cold excitement which gave her gooseflesh. She put the pieces of paper away carefully in her bag. 'I must pretend to know nothing,' she said to herself—and suddenly was assailed by the dread that Venetia's action might turn out to be an isolated one, which could never be brought home to her. I must pray for her and for Toby, she thought with absolute sincerity and, at the same moment, was wondering where she could get hold of more damaging proofs of Venetia's infidelity, for from the first moment of her discovery she assumed that Venetia could only be concealing her visit to Swindon because of a criminal relationship with a man. Criminal! If Venetia was a criminal, no excuse and no forgiveness was possible. Angela wondered whether she should embark on amateur detective enquiries at Swindon, but she decided that she must be careful not to allow Venetia to suspect that her sordid intrigue—for surely it could be nothing else—had been discovered—or to inform Toby prematurely. Venetia would dig her own grave, and she must have time to dig it deep enough. Angela

44

made up her mind to check up on Venetia's appointment with the dentist. It would excite no suspicions if she were to ring up and say: 'Mrs. Barnard isn't quite sure whether she posted her letter about the appointment with Mr. Dalrymple'—and then if it turned out that there were no record of an appointment for that week, she would say: 'Oh, that's all right then. She asked me to cancel it, if the letter had accidentally been posted.'

From that moment, Angela maintained a relentless watch—noting that at breakfast Venetia thrust a letter into her pocket quickly, instead of opening it and reading it while she ate and leaving it lying upon the table as was her custom. And that afternoon, among the letters waiting for the postman to take, was one addressed to Carlo Marx, Esq., Widdicombe's Circus, Bristol. For a moment Angela thought of purloining it, and steaming it open. But she resisted the temptation. It might be premature. Venetia might not yet have committed adultery. That night, Angela prayed sincerely that she might do what was right and not allow herself to judge her erring sister. After all, even if she could prove that Venetia were criminal and Toby were to divorce her, she could not ever bring herself to marry a divorced man. That very fact was enough to ensure that her motives were disinterested. Much to Angela's regret, she had to return to work in Toby's London office before she had found out anything further—and she had no knowledge for certain when she would be returning to The Old Forge. All sorts of things might happen in her absence.

Angela's departure was a relief, particularly to Toby, who had noticed something frozen and self-conscious in her behaviour during the last three days of her stay.

4

TOBY did not ask any questions about the visit to the dentist. But Venetia felt enveloped in unspoken questions which she could not have answered, and about which she must make up her mind. Toby merely seemed depressed and, as she was feeling guilty, his depression made her long to escape from him. When the time came it seemed astonishing that she should simply get into her own car and drive it to Bristol. The feeling of boredom and guilt, of having to face problems and make decisions, was suddenly swept away when she saw Carlo waiting for her in the car park where they had arranged to meet. No past history of mistakes, misunderstandings, faults on both sides, and bitterness swallowed down for the sake of peace! All clean, fresh as the sea: the eager eyes of a lover to whom she owed nothing.

They picnicked in a lonely wood above Clifton and, as Carlo cautiously released the cork of the bottle of champagne which she had taken out of the wine cellar, she wondered for a moment if Toby would miss it, and when she would own up to having taken it. But she did not tell Carlo that the wine was Toby's when he made eyes at her, and told her that she was taking him out of his class. They laughed a lot as they made love.

After the afternoon performance, they went to a dance hall and danced for the whole evening. And when they went to bed afterwards they talked about dancing until they fell asleep. The extraordinary thing was that, though they danced as though they were two halves of one creature, they disagreed profoundly with each other on the subject.

Indeed they disagreed so much that when, next morning after breakfast, Carlo began talking, it was a relief that he did not choose to continue the discussion. His first words were 'Circus overheads'. Venetia thought he was explaining about the arrangements necessary for putting up tightropes, and swinging trapezes in the Big Top: then she realized that he was talking about money, and she tried to listen intelligently.

'When the circus closes down it goes back to the home farm, and the ponies go out to grass . . . but the sea-lions have to get their three or four stone of herring apiece—and a swimming-pool. Elephant overheads depend on the price of hay—usually between seven and twenty pounds a ton: then they need a covered yard, and a stable with heating in winter. The big cats are damned expensive—the knacker for meat and the vet all the time, and then insurance is high. So, when we are resting, salaries are cut, but of course the animals have to be kept in

48

training—so it was a lean time for Poulenc. One year he was really broke. Then he got a chance to make some money on the side—and that just saved him. An American girl turned up, name of Judie. She was the daughter of one of the well-known egg-heads: Dean of a college somewhere in the States. Well she got herself engaged to an Indian Rajah. She said that her fiancé had a thing about tigers. She thought that if he saw her working Poulenc's tigers it would do the trick, and she could pull off the marriage. It looked like the Rajah had started to cool off, and it needed tigers to bring him on again. At first she proposed a lump payment, after the Rajah married her—but Poulenc wasn't standing for that one. But in the end she settled for ten guineas a lesson, and three lessons a week. Judie learned so fast that it seemed like she'd been born with the know-how. She was a fat jolly kid. When she laughed, you couldn't see her eyes. Just buried in fat. Everyone liked her: lions and tigers and all—do anything for her. She was no end keen, and it didn't take more than three weeks before she could get them out in the big cage and work them alone. After that, she kept trying to date up the Rajah to come and watch. But each time he rang up and said he couldn't make it that day. Poulenc could tell there was some funny business there. Then, one day, Judie brought him along with her. He was a small, monkey-faced chap: dark skin, dark suit, old school tie, with very nice manners. Judie introduced Poulenc and me—and went off to change, and we sat down to watch. She put on a really good show, but the Rajah sat there with a disgusted sort of look on his face. When it was over, and she was changing back, he thanked Poulenc for looking after her so well. He said he had been really anxious about her.

' "Judie's such a sweet girl. Only, if you will excuse me saying so, she has this unfortunate obsession about tigers. I find it very embarrassing." He seemed uncertain if he should go on. He didn't know if he could trust us. We said nothing. But whatever it was, he had to say it before Judie came out of the dressing-room.

' "I was a little bit in love with her. She may have told you that we were almost engaged to be married. Then I found out about these tigers . . . she only likes me because she associates a Rajput Prince with tigers . . . it's too childish. I wouldn't have a tiger within fifty miles . . . I'm terrified of them. But she won't believe me. She keeps talking about the jungle and tigers. . . . I live in Rome and Cairo and the Italian Riviera."

' Judie came out, they drove off, and Poulenc started laughing and laughing. When he got through with that he said: "I can't go on charging Judie ten guineas an afternoon for working my tigers when it's pushing her marriage into the never-never land."

' Next day he told her: "You'd do better to give

up coming here. Never mention a tiger to your Rajah again. He's terrified of them. He told me."

'"Do you think I didn't know that?" said Judie. "Of course he's scared stiff of them. That's the thing he's got: I told you about it, he's a masochist with a streak of the sadist voyeur. I'll lend you a book that will explain it all, if you don't know about sex. It's a wonderful subject if you really dig into it. If you knew about it, you'd understand that, being a masochist and a crypto sadist, it gives him the most tremendous kick to see me in the cage."

'Poulenc told her there had been no sign of a kick while the Rajah was watching her. Her gen about him was wrong and she had better not waste any more of her money. But she begged to be allowed to keep on working the cats. She certainly had a thing about tigers, like the Rajah said. About a fortnight later, Judie showed up in tears. She said it was the finish: Monkey-face had broken it off: he had written to tell her it was useless for them to meet again: he had left for Cairo. She had spent all her money: suicide was the only way out . . . but she had come to kiss the tigers good-bye. And she went straight into the cages and started to do just that.

Poulenc thought she was on the level, so he took her on as a kennel maid. She stayed with him for nearly six months until she had earned back nearly all the money he had had off her. Then she went back to the States and got a job in a Zoo.'

'I should like to meet your friend Poulenc again,' said Venetia. 'We owe him a lot. If he hadn't taken me into that tiger's cage, I shouldn't be here now.'

'I had better come clean about that tiger cage racket,' said Carlo.

'What do you mean?'

'That offer to take a lady from the audience into a tiger's cage was a publicity racket I had thought up. It was wonderful publicity because no woman ever accepted it, and they all talked about it for the rest of their lives. You were the first and only. . . . I must have made the offer to over three hundred women before I struck you. Then, as you were game to go in, I had to go on with it. Was I sweating all the time you were in the cage! And I bloody nearly got fired because I let you go in. I would have done, except Poulenc said it was all his doing. After that the boss put a stop to my offer, because the insurance premium would have cost the earth.'

'Why didn't you tell me before?' asked Venetia, not knowing whether she was pleased or angry.

'I was going to tell you at Lady Ida's. Then I thought better of it. You see now, why I said it was kismet. . . . You were the one and only woman to call my hand, and then I found myself sitting right beside you.'

Venetia drove back slowly to The Old Forge. She thought she had scarcely ever been happier. How absurd that anything so simple should be supposed to make her feel guilty. Carlo and Toby, Carlo and Sebastian belonged to entirely different worlds. They were on different planets. Her love for them did not overlap: it was different in kind, not simply in degree.

'Just because their worlds do not touch at any point I cannot feel guilty,' she decided.

But on her return the concealment of her movements and of her love, and the lies told or implied, became intensely disagreeable. It seemed to her that even if Toby had not already guessed the truth, he was waiting for her to tell it to him. Several times she went out of her way to make up to him for her infidelity. Curiously enough it was easier for her to make love to Toby, and to abandon herself wholly to the enjoyment of his love, since Carlo had made her feel happy and enriched. When Toby made love to her there was no thrill of excitement, but there was a dream-like, peaceful sensuality. Toby quietened her restlessness, filled her with contentment and allayed her fears of conscience that she might be hurting him. To conceal her love for Carlo and to deceive Toby, at a time when she most wanted to make up to him with love for not being in love, filled her with distress.

For Carlo the invitation to Lady Ida's party had been like crossing to a new watershed in the mountains, and perceiving an unsuspected valley, luxuriant with a new climate, rich in grapes and peaches, lying below him. All his life he had existed, kept his place and slowly risen by toughness and incessant alertness. In the world he knew, there was no repose, no trust, no time for self-revelation. The Darwinian law of the devil take the hindmost summed up its philosophy. And suddenly he crossed, though only momentarily, into a genial region where the inhabitants appeared to repose on billowing clouds of mutual goodwill, where they all took one another on trust. Not that he was sucker enough to believe it was quite that.

No sooner had he realized that this new world might become open to him than the most lovely woman in it sought him out and took him as her lover. He was intoxicated by her; he was in love with her—as much as he had ever been in his life, and yet he only occasionally thought of her as an individual. For though he was in love with her, she stood for all the women of the happy valley; she typified and was confused in the whole class of rich and leisured women. Carlo saw himself as a conquistador who had penetrated single-handed into Eldorado. He felt no astonishment that he should have done so: nothing that little Carlo did in that line could surprise him: he knew his qualities. But he was astonished that there had been no guards upon the frontier, no passport demanded, that there were no bouncers to chuck him out. Instead of that, there had been Venetia, driving her own car, disposing of her own person, to welcome him with love. Carlo would have liked to have felt the conquistador's contempt for the inhabitants of the happy valley, but Venetia's dancing won his immediate respect. He was far more impressed by her dancing than by her beauty: they were both 'one hundred per cent', but the first commanded its price in Carlo's world, the classic second did not quite belong there.

Between performances, Carlo worked in a long caravan fitted as an office and linked with temporary telephones to the outside world. Men were constantly entering, to shout an order or a question, or to ask a favour. One of his duties was to keep informed of the changes which the ringmaster was constantly making in the performances. There was always some acrobat who had strained a muscle, elephant or lioness coming into season, clown dolefully anxious to attend a funeral. While Carlo worked, his thoughts were filled with Venetia. It was her negative qualities that he tended to dwell on, for they distinguished her from all the women who had 'sent' him in the past. They had been of two types: those whose instinct it was to exploit the male at the moment when he was weakest—just before and just after their surrender—and those who were willing to sacrifice all personal independence and self-respect, so long as they could attach themselves like limpets to a man. The pride of the first class was measured in what they could extract from the lover of the moment, that of the second in their abject subjection and enslavement to him. Venetia, as he had seen at once, belonged to neither category. She asked nothing but sincerity and gave nothing that she might not be free to take away.

Carlo saw these spiritual differences clearly, though he would not have been willing to accept them, had not Venetia intoxicated him. Her clothes, her scent, her voice, her car and her handling of it, all these were a 'a hundred per cent'. But above all, she made love and accepted his love with an eagerness untinged by any ulterior motive, or by triumph or regret. And was she 'a hundred per cent' in bed! She 'sent' him . . . to regions undreamed of . . . she made all other women . . .

For all these reasons Carlo made up his mind that as soon as he could straighten out his tangles, he would get her away from her lame duck. With Venetia behind him, he might go places. He might make a bigger mark in pictures than in the circus, or he might start a dance hall. Rock 'n' roll was a passing fad, and when fashion turned back, as it always did, he and Venetia might be the Astaires of the future. Carlo had read about them.

5

ONE morning, when Toby woke up, he found that Venetia was awake, leaning upon her elbow and looking at him. He put his arm round her and drew her to him, but she shook her head, pushing him away. This refusal of the habitual embrace in which he enfolded her before throwing himself out of bed, was unusual and startled him. He turned his back, fixed his leg, went into the bathroom and dressed hurriedly, anxious to busy his thoughts with something which had nothing to do with Venetia.

A few minutes later he was astonished to find her standing beside him in her dressing-gown. He turned to her and she put her hands lightly on his shoulders and looked into his face with an expression of acute unhappiness, and then looked away quickly.

'Why not speak? You had much better tell me,' he said, and as he uttered the words the knowledge of what she was going to say, if she did speak, chilled him. Venetia said nothing. She moved slightly, as though in despair, and let her hands fall lifelessly from his shoulders.

'You had much better tell me,' he repeated.

She lifted her face and looked at him tenderly, her eyes moist with tears.

'I'm in love . . . I think I have fallen in love,' she said at last, in a low voice.

'I knew it. . . . Who with?' said Toby.

Venetia hesitated and then, making an effort, said in a flat voice: 'With Carlo . . . Carlo Marx . . . the man who danced with me at Lady Ida's.'

'I knew it,' said Toby quietly. A wave of intense pity for her came over him. He knew that her marriage with him left her unsatisfied, after all these years. That she had no outlet for her beauty and her talents, that she deserved far more than she got from him, or that he could give her—but that she should now fall in love with a man who, he was certain, was in all ways her inferior filled him with despairing pity. It was cruelty. A horrible trick was being played upon her. Somehow or other he must hide this knowledge from her, and they must make the best of it.

'I will do all I can to help you. It won't be easy for me. But I will try to help you, and not to hurt you.'

Venetia put her arms round his neck. She was crying.

'There is no one: no one in the world like you. Nobody is as kind as you.' She spoke with a simple conviction, completely accepting the truth of what he had said.

Toby put his arms round her and her head fell on to his shoulder. Holding her tight and close to him was good. But something kept hammering in his head with the message: 'I mustn't think. I mustn't let myself think.'

'Come and drink some coffee,' he said.

'No questions. I mustn't cross-examine,' he said to himself, for his first impulse was to drag all the details out of her. Presently Venetia gave him some of them of her own accord.

'I went to Swindon that time when I said I was going to London, and I stayed the night with him at an hotel so that the circus people should not know about us. Since then I've seen him again. At Bristol when I said I was going to the dentist. I've told him I will meet him again when the circus moves to Gloucester.'

Toby nodded and deliberately buttered a piece of toast. He was living in an unreal world.

During that morning, Toby's sense of the ironic pathos of Venetia's having fallen in love with a man so absolutely unworthy of her saved him from going deeper into his own feelings.

'It can't last for very long,' was his first reaction. 'She is the most faithful creature in the world, and having given her love will not easily change. But, even so, she cannot go on being in love with that hair-creamed, greasy black head and that awful cockney accent.'

Toby did not know that every husband who finds out that his wife has been unfaithful believes her lover to be unworthy of her and is astonished at her choice.

Although during the following weeks Toby was to experience many violently contradictory emotions, he never felt inclined to blame Venetia for falling in love with another man, or to reproach her for treacherously taking him as her lover. Fortunately for him, he never thought that he was being wronged: only that he was being made to suffer. It never occurred to him to wonder if he should forgive her: there was nothing to forgive, since he really believed that she was free to love without interference from him. This idea was however modified by his assumption that falling in love was an involuntary act, and caused by physical conditions of which she was unconscious.

Toby's jealousy was thus directed at her lover, or showed itself in fear that her love affair would make it impossible for his marriage to continue. Either she would leave him for Carlo, or he would find the pain of living with her unendurable. If only Carlo could be removed all might be well. And his thoughts immediately turned to devising plans for his removal. It had to be what the detective writers called 'the perfect murder', and Toby felt fairly confident that he could devise one. Germs in the gum of a reply-paid envelope ought to be difficult to trace —Carlo would infect himself heavily with a concentrated culture of anthrax, or something of that sort, and would have posted off the incriminating evidence before he got ill. Poisoned chocolates would not do at all: he would probably give one to Venetia. But though poison, or germs, were the obvious way to commit a safe murder, it would provide no emotional satisfaction. What Toby longed to do was to hit Carlo very hard with some weapon like a hammer, on the temple or the side of the head, to see the blood spurt out and the body fall. Toby remembered the strange feeling of satisfied surprise which he had always experienced after he had killed a man at close quarters. Unlike most R.A.F. pilots, he had been engaged in hand-to-hand fighting on three occasions, and each time he had killed his man. He could shoot Carlo, and if he used an old-fashioned flintlock horse pistol, it would give the experts something to think about. Only violent killing, at close quarters, would enable him to forget Venetia's infidelity. Moreover, he suspected that if he committed a 'perfect murder' by post, he would find himself difficult to live with. The memories of the Germans whom he had killed during the war had never troubled him. There was a better reason for murdering Carlo than there had been for killing them—his own happiness and the future of his life with Venetia. But however repugnant poisoning might be, it would be better than a bungling bloody affray ending on the gallows, or in Broadmoor.

'I would certainly like to kill him—and it would not be difficult to contrive an accident in which he met his death, if he plays about with tigers,' Toby often said to himself. But apart from any scruples about murder, or fears of being found out, there were two sides to the question.

'If I killed him I should perhaps break Venetia's heart. Even if she never suspected me of the murder, how could I stand the strain of living with her and trying to console her? I care more about her happiness than my own. So the paradox arises that I cannot kill him so long as she is in love with him—and when she is no longer in love with him, killing him becomes unnecessary.'

Toby laughed at this thought but he could not dismiss his loathing of Carlo. While he was with Venetia, he could usually manage to control his thoughts—but when he was alone, the image of the circus man making love to her, of her physical ecstasy clasping that other man's body, obsessed him.

For many years Toby had concealed nothing from Venetia: now it came to him as a shock to realize that he must conceal almost everything. He must try to hide his jealousy, his loathing for Carlo, the murderous feeling in his heart, and the pity he felt for her because of her choice of such an unworthy lover.

Both Venetia and Toby had originally got the impression that Carlo was the lion-tamer's assistant, and although Venetia had discovered her mistake, she had not explained that Carlo's present work in the circus was that of publicity.

As a result of his misapprehension, Toby spent many of the hours when he was lying between waking and sleeping in devising treacherous methods of getting wild beasts to tear Carlo in pieces. Then, as these fantasies tended to disgust him, he introduced alternatives in which he tested his own courage by going into the animals' cage himself. He soon, however, became nauseated by the silliness and futility of his own imaginings, but a recognition of their nature did not make them less violent, or less frequent.

To suit Carlo, who was busiest on Saturday, Venetia had fixed upon a Friday for her visit to Gloucester. This, unfortunately, was the day upon which Angela was, at short notice, bringing down a French aircraft designer for the week-end.

As Venetia was leaving the house, she saw Toby standing waiting to intercept her. He was trying to suppress his agitation and to be reasonable. This resulted in his adopting a rather stilted manner which exasperated her.

'Don't forget that D' 'enson will be here about eight. What about dinner?'

'It's laid on. Anyway I shall be back in time to see about it,' said Venetia crossly.

'Is his room ready?'

'Mrs. Ball is doing it out this morning. Must you really fuss about these things?'

Toby pretended not to hear her.

'One other thing. Will you buy a bottle of whisky? These French people have a craze for whisky in preference to their own drinks. See if you can get a pure malt. Otherwise Irish, John Power's Three Swallows ten year old. Have you enough money to pay for it?'

Venetia nodded her head. She was furious with Toby for inventing these domestic excuses in order to come out and watch her departure with an expression of high tragedy on his face.

'It would serve him right if I stayed away the whole week-end,' she said to herself as she drove off, feeling conscious that he was watching the car going down the gravel drive.

Before she reached Worcester it began to rain: she had no reserved room to which she and Carlo could go, he did not want to take her to his caravan, and they drove off together in a silence which was new in their relationship.

'I told Toby that I was in love with you,' said Venetia suddenly.

Carlo started in his seat.

'That means I've got to watch out for trouble. What the hell made you tell him?'

'It was impossible to go on hiding it. Moreover, I have decided on a policy of complete honesty.'

'Honesty at my expense. . . . What do you think he is likely to do?'

'He was quite extraordinary. He said he would do all he could to help and would try not to hurt me.'

Carlo was suspicious of this. He could not understand it and wanted time to think it over.

'If that is on the level, it means we needn't lose any sleep over him,' he said.

'You certainly need not, and I never expected you to,' replied Venetia, speaking to him more coldly than she had ever done before.

They said no more about Toby, but twenty minutes later, when they had found a suitable place and were lying together high up on a stack of baled clover in a Dutch barn, Carlo said before he began making love to her:

'If you are going to be on the level, I shall have to be too. I've got to pull out one that you won't like. I never told you that I'm married.'

'Is your wife in love with you?' asked Venetia. She wanted to ask: 'Are you in love with her?' but she was too proud, and the words would not come.

'I wouldn't know. She says she's not. But I think she is really,' Carlo replied. He felt that he was out of his depth in strange waters, but he was determined to go on, excited and attracted at the possibility of a relationship new to him.

'Tell me something about her.'

'She's a trapeze artiste. I think she's one of the

world's winners. She puts her career first and all the time, naturally. She's in Stockholm now. She's Spanish, and our spot of bother is that she's a Roman Catholic and that I'm not. If she found out about you, she would do something to spoil your beauty. So I shan't be on the level with her. That's the reason why I refused to let you come to my caravan. All circus people have a passion for making mischief. Rows and jealousies are the breath of life to them. They get bored so easily. Besides, a lot of them are very moral about this sort of thing. It would take a lot to explain circus mentality. I study it all the time, and, d'you know, it's fascinating.'

There was an eager intelligence in Carlo which surprised and delighted Venetia. His mind was adaptable and growing. He had an interest in people's motives which might take him far. She did not admit that the fact of his marriage had upset her—but it had, because she wanted him to be more dependent on her. Toby had done much to make her what she was: she wanted a lover who would owe her everything and whose mind she would form. Nor could she blind herself entirely to a streak of insensitiveness in Carlo. A little later he said:

'There's always some trouble to a marriage. Mine's not really so bad as yours.'

'Why do you think I'm so unlucky?'

'You ought to have your name in lights. And

you're living in the country, married to a cripple with one foot.'

'Toby was a beautiful dancing partner when I married him.'

'Well, that was tough. But now he's one of these smashed-up R.A.F. types. Why doesn't he wear handle-bar moustaches?'

'Toby was a physicist—he did pure science before he went into the R.A.F. His research on air-flow helped to make supersonic speed possible.'

Carlo laughed. 'Gosh, I didn't know you were so proud of being married to a real egg-head.'

'I suppose I am proud because Toby has a brilliant intellect. But, in a way, that has been the trouble in our marriage. I can't understand his work, or help him. And all the time I feel it's there, filling up most of his mind. More and more I have felt that he looks on me as a child with whom he is in love— but who can't be taken seriously. He hasn't noticed that my life has grown empty and emptier. Women can't all be artists. I once hoped to be a dancer. But it wouldn't matter sacrificing that, if I could have expressed myself through him. Women can create a man; can make him succeed, or make him realize himself. I can't do that with Toby: it's the other way; he has made me what I am. Our marriage has been a failure just because he is so brilliant, or because he wants so little from me.'

Venetia paused. She could not go on and say that

she hoped—that she had hoped . . . that she could find an outlet for creative activity in Carlo. But if only he would say something which showed that he understood and cared, and was eager to accept what she was offering!

There was a pause and she waited, feeling that on his words the future of their relationship depended.

'I guess that explains his shooting the line about trying to help you, and not wanting to hurt you. That's one hundred per cent egg-head,' said Carlo. Then, noticing her expression, which was of infinite despair, he said:

'I must be dumb to talk,' and took her passive, unresisting body into his arms.

That afternoon in the haybarn, covered in the broken clover, hay and dust, Venetia got rid of her resentment by making love to Carlo with a frenzy that left both of them shattered and exhausted. She felt scarcely alive when Carlo looked at his watch and she found that she would be late getting back. It was a long drive on wet, crooked roads, and that evening she took many chances.

Toby was hobbling about, waiting for her.

'Did you get the whisky?'

'No. I forgot it.'

Toby could not suppress his annoyance. 'You might have remembered the only thing I asked you to do.'

They walked in silence into the drawing-room; Toby sat down and said:

'I wanted to avoid seeing you when you got back. I don't want to go into what I have been feeling.'

'I didn't want to see you either—but only because I'm in such a dishevelled state,' said Venetia, who remained standing. Toby looked at her face streaked with dirt, and her hair full of bits of hay.

'I suppose you drove him out into the country and found some place under a hedge,' he said.

'Yes. In a haybarn. He told me that he was married.'

Toby's heart leaped with joy.

'Is she in the circus too?'

'She's a trapeze girl. But she's in Stockholm. I gather they have rather a hell of a time because she's a Roman Catholic and he isn't.'

There was a pause.

'He doesn't want me to go and live with him, because circus people are so jealous and he has a lot on his hands. So I told him I didn't want to leave you.'

'Have you been wanting to leave me?' asked Toby.

'Surely you must understand what it is to be in love? I want to be with him all the time,' said Venetia in a tone of cold exasperation.

'What about Sebastian? Surely it would upset him terribly if you went to live with *him* in a circus?'

'I thought that is what we were talking about.'

'You said that you didn't want to leave me at present.'

'When I said *you* I meant Sebastian. But what are you going on like this for? Haven't I told you that I'm not going? That I'll make that sacrifice.'

'Sacrifice?'

'Oh, I'm sorry if I used the wrong word.'

'When I had that affair with Emerald, I never dreamed for one moment of leaving you and the boy. When I was offered the job in India, I refused it because it would have meant exile for you and only seeing Sebastian at long intervals,' said Toby in an unnatural flat voice.

'But the position is quite different. You are in love with me. You have always been in love with me. I'm not in love with you. You know that, don't you?'

Venetia left the room and Toby sat motionless staring in front of him. Movement of any sort had somehow become impossible, and he felt paralysed and frightened. Venetia's callousness had been an unexpected shock. He wondered for a time whether it would not be best—indeed the only thing—to divorce her. It was obvious that if Venetia felt like that they could not live together. Toby wondered whether he was not in something like a cataleptic trance, but he could do nothing to wake himself out of it. He ought to move, but he could not make the effort of will to do so.

He had been sitting motionless for nearly twenty minutes when Venetia came back into the room, and looked at him with surprise.

'Is there something wrong?'

Toby looked at her but did not speak.

'What has upset you? I was only trying to be honest.'

What had upset him? If she could not guess, it would be hard to explain.

'I know you were being honest. That is the upsetting thing. You really would be happy if I were to die at once.'

'Don't dramatize things.'

'It's not necessary. They are dramatic enough already,' he replied quietly. Then, making a great effort of will, he unclasped his hand and took hold of his chair and slowly managed to stand up. Venetia left the room, and Toby hobbled about busying himself in putting out glasses, finding the gin and the French. Then he went to the kitchen to get a lemon and ice out of the refrigerator. Since there was no whisky, he would give D'Argenson a dry Martini. But before he had got back with them, there was the sound of the crunch of tyres on the gravel, the front door was thrown open and the hall filled with the loud noise of Angela talking fluent French.

'*Où êtes-vous, Toby? Monsieur D'Argenson*

réclame le whisky! Il faut que je deballe la bouteille que j'ai apportée dans ma serviette.'

So Angela, with her characteristic forethought, had saved them, and with her vitality and command of the language would enable them to get through the evening.

'God bless Angela. She's saved us,' exclaimed Venetia, as Toby went into the bedroom nearly four hours later and picked up his pyjamas.

'I shall sleep in Sebastian's room,' he said.

'Don't be an owl. The bed isn't made up. You won't sleep, and you won't be fit to deal with your Frenchman in the morning.'

'I don't suppose I shall. But it can't be helped.'

'Come in here,' and, giving him a curiously quizzical look, Venetia patted the sheet beside her.

Toby gazed at her dumbly. All the evening the decision about a divorce had been fermenting at the back of his mind.

'Don't be an owl. We are both absolutely emotionally exhausted, and we shall only make ourselves ill unless we get some sleep. You'll sleep much better here.'

Five minutes later Venetia cuddled close beside him when he got into bed, and immediately fell fast asleep. Toby lay awake. He continually tried to summarize what he should say to D'Argenson, who was being difficult about modifications required for tropical countries, but his mind skidded and he rehearsed again and again the words, and the tones in which Venetia had spoken them, when she had got back that evening. Eventually he fell into a dream in which Venetia and a tiger and an aircraft from which pieces kept breaking off and flying past the cockpit, as it slowly disintegrated in the air, were impossible to disentangle.

D'Argenson and Angela left the following day, and after their departure Toby reverted to his day-dreams of revenge. He had almost decided in favour of diving an aircraft and escaping by parachute, leaving Carlo to crash, when he suddenly had a new idea.

'Why run any risk? I can buy him off. I can offer him a thousand pounds on condition that he signs a document agreeing never to see Venetia again.'

Toby was delighted with his idea. No money could be better spent. Of course Carlo might refuse the offer out of mere vanity, or *amour propre*. Or he might refuse because he rightly guessed that he could get more in the long run by bringing about a divorce, and then marrying Venetia. Toby had got so far as to wonder what he would sell to raise the cash, when it occurred to him that, if Venetia discovered that her lover had thrown her over for a payment of money, she might commit suicide. Perhaps she would never speak to him again, if she knew he had offered the bribe. All the same the idea of buying the man off

73

enchanted Toby. It had the immense merit of degrading all three parties, whereas a murder would invest them with the spurious grandeur of tragedy. With what overwhelming contempt would he write out the cheque! With what unanswerable logic would he show it to Venetia when it came back from the bank with Carlo's endorsement upon it!

But Venetia would never lift up her head again . . . and he could not endure to hurt her. Probably it would have to be murder after all . . . a carefully contrived accident.

The circus was booked for a week each at Birmingham and Manchester, and a fortnight at Blackpool and Colwyn Bay. If Venetia were to continue to live with Toby it would be impossible for her to see Carlo every week. As a result the lovers wrote to each other almost every other day. Toby was always down before Venetia in the morning, and took a perverse pleasure in picking out Carlo's letter, pinching it to see if it held one sheet or three or four, and then taking it immediately to Venetia, wherever she might be.

Separation from her lover, while thinking continually about love and excited by his letters, led to Venetia's being unexpectedly kind to Toby. Putting her arms on his shoulders when they were alone together after lunch, she looked at him and said:

'Come along. It will make us both much happier.'

'Don't be unselfish about this,' said Toby. 'I don't want acts of charity.'

'You make me blush,' replied Venetia, and Toby saw that she was actually blushing. Such occasions multiplied. Love was deliberate, though wholehearted, on Venetia's side; it was almost hysterically emotional on Toby's.

The thought that he was sharing his wife with another man, and that to do so was dishonourable and in some way unfair, came to him often. Surely he should have the strength to renounce her? And Toby was surprised that Venetia seemed to feel nothing of the kind. 'How can she want two men?' he asked himself, although he had often wanted two women himself. He had not the strength to refuse her love if it were possible to gain it, and each time it seemed also a secret victory over his rival. But though Toby quickly became shameless, and felt he had no pride left, he did not so easily shed the vanity which made him constantly wonder: 'Is she always comparing me with Carlo to my disadvantage? What does she think of him as a lover?'

For this reason Toby was only happy if he could produce an ultimate physical ecstasy in Venetia. She, on her side, set herself to achieve the same. At such moments she was making up for a great many different things: for making Toby unhappy; for Carlo's absence; for the love she had often denied herself in the past.

Though love-making affected them differently, it drew them close and enabled them to see clearly, without resentment, into each other's hearts. They grew steadily more wrapped up in each other. Carlo, it seemed, was functioning as the catalyst of their love. Toby's passion meant comfort for Venetia, but the peace of mind, the rest he gave her, was not to be distinguished from the size of his limbs, and the weight of his body. And, with the physical relief of love, was the sly pleasure of feeling that she now dominated the man who, for so many years, had dominated her.

As Toby and she made love more often, and her physical desire was satisfied, her feelings for Carlo underwent an unconscious change. At first a dancing partner, he had rapidly become a passionate lover kindling excitement, and awakening a sense of youth and of power. As she drew closer to Toby, Carlo began to awaken her maternal instincts: she longed to form him, to educate him, to launch him on the road to success, to refine his sensibilities.

Toby came out of the storm of physical passion clear-eyed. Once indeed he asked himself whether this heightened relationship and intimacy with Venetia was not worth all the tortures of jealousy and fear of losing her. He could reflect: Being cuckolded has involved me in a second honeymoon.

And then, with his physical desire gratified, he could see himself and his jealousy with detachment.

76

One day after beginning to brood, as usual, on murder and revenge, he was able to say to himself:

'I won't accept these emotions which are being imposed on me. They are too high a price to pay. Whether Venetia stays or goes, whether she keeps me or rejects me as her lover, I shall henceforward be myself. I cannot and will not allow myself to be turned into a maniac. All these homicidal emotions are foreign to me. I shall rid myself of them—and the best, the only way to set about it, is to think, as I did at the first minute, when she told me, only of her happiness, putting that before everything and realizing that she is the sole judge of what it may be. I cannot expect my wife to choose her lover to suit my taste. Of course he is unworthy. But should I be happier if he were a man I respected? I should feel far less hate—but then I should have far less hope. And I should be in the intolerable position of having to force myself to be on some sort of terms with him. I need never see or speak to this little super in the circus, with his cockney accent and cock-sparrow inferiority complex. All that matters is that Venetia should be happy, and if I can add to her happiness I shall not feel wholly despicable.'

6

VENETIA decided to join Carlo for three days
during the week that the circus was moving to Manchester. When she told Toby, he said nothing,
but marked the dates when she would be away
in his diary. After that they avoided speaking
about it, until one morning when Venetia was
having breakfast in bed, Toby came into the bedroom.

'The school secretary has just telephoned to say
that three of the boys have got polio, and that the
doctors advise dispersal to prevent an epidemic. So
all the boys who have homes to go to are being sent
home for what is left of this term. They are putting
Sebastian on the first train this morning, and we
must meet him in Newbury this afternoon. I'm
afraid it may mean that you won't be able to go to
Manchester after all.'

'Oh, damn,' said Venetia, sitting straight up in
bed. 'Damn, damn, damn, damn, damn. I suppose
I shan't.'

'I'm so sorry, darling. But I don't see how . . .'
began Toby, but Venetia cut him short.

'Don't put on such a hypocritical look of smug

sorrow. You come and tell me this, looking like the undertaker's man. Go away, for God's sake.'

Toby went out of the room and shut the door, but a moment afterwards he opened it again and went back.

'I forgot. Here's a letter from *him*.' He threw it on the bed and retreated.

'I'm sorry I was so bad-tempered,' she said, going into his office an hour later. 'But it is maddening, as Carlo had got leave for the whole three days and I had planned to explore the Yorkshire dales. . . . But I see it can't be helped. I hope to goodness Sebastian's all right. I don't suppose there's any danger for him, do you? I'll go and meet him this afternoon.' Her face expressed a sudden horror and terror. It seemed extraordinary that that should not have been her first reaction.

Toby sat and thought for some time. He was full of terror about Sebastian's safety, but all the same his heart was dancing with delight at Venetia's trip having to be cancelled. The thought of Carlo in Manchester with three days hanging on his hands, unable to see Venetia, was particularly delightful. Toby took one of his best cigars out of its box, lit it, and sat gloating.

'Why shouldn't the little bastard come down here?' he suddenly asked himself. The question was agony: the pain of it almost physical, but he pursued it. 'We couldn't have him staying in the house—

80

but he could be somewhere in the neighbourhood, and Venetia could get away for the afternoon with him . . . so long as Sebastian doesn't guess what's in the wind . . . we must fix it so that he doesn't. Why the hell do I think of things like this? It hasn't even occurred to Venetia as a possibility.'

Toby sat and chewed his cigar irresolutely for ten minutes, then he got up and went in search of his wife. Venetia was writing a letter to Carlo, and lifted a proud and angry mask at the interruption.

'I'm sorry to butt in. But I've got a suggestion to make. I think we might give a large party. We can ask all the friends we know in Wiltshire to come over. We'll have the swimming-pool all lit up, and dancing. And it wouldn't look odd to Sebastian, or to anyone else, if you invited *him* to come to it. *He* could stay in Reading, or somewhere, and you could get away for the afternoon next day to see *him*.'

Venetia sprang up from her seat while he was still speaking, and flung her arms round his neck.

'Toby. You sometimes are quite extraordinary . . . the kindest man in the whole world. You are too good to me and I . . .' She was weeping, and Toby found the violence of her emotion painful to contemplate.

'Don't be silly. That's settled then.' He began gently disengaging himself from her embrace, as he added:

'I'll write out a card and tell Angela to get it

81

printed and send it out. We'll make out a list at lunch . . .' He went rather hurriedly out of the room, while he still had control of his voice. Venetia's tears seemed to be infectious.

Both Sebastian and his mother arrived home from the station in wild spirits and began shouting for Toby before they had even got out of the car.

He went out to meet them, blinking a little in the sunlight, and smiling at the excitement. Sebastian was shouting:

'Clean . . . Come clean . . .'

With their flushed cheeks, blue-black hair and big, almond-shaped blue eyes mother and son were astonishingly alike. Indeed it would almost be possible, thought Toby, to mistake Sebastian for Venetia if you were to dress him in her clothes. . . . A twinge of pain like toothache went through him, as he realized how terribly much Venetia must be in love to have ever wanted to leave Sebastian. 'But she didn't, she only said she would make the sacrifice and not leave him . . .' he reminded himself. Meanwhile both of them were shouting at him something about a secret.

'I've kept it. I've kept the secret, although he began twisting my arm while I was driving,' called Venetia.

'Come clean. I shall bash you. I shall smash you, squash you in a folio and give you both polio, and I'll go on hunger strike rather than come and live with parents who keep secrets. Come clean, Toby.'

But Toby stared so blankly that Venetia felt a tremor of terror, and began to say:

'Tell him your great idea for next week . . .'

But Toby was already smiling.

'We are going to give an immense party, there will be oceans of champagne and acres of smoked salmon, bushels of wood strawberries; the swimming-pool illuminated, the lawn floodlit, fire balloons, rockets and maroons, all the pretty girls and titled people in Wiltshire, your mother singing extremely improper French songs, and thrilling stories told by one of the best storytellers in the world.'

'Good God! Where do you get the money?' cried Sebastian.

'Money is no object with your father. If the lawn were large enough I should have the Household Cavalry doing a musical ride,' boasted Toby. Sebastian was impressed.

Invitations for the party were sent out, wine ordered from London, Angela commissioned to choose delicacies, and see that they arrived in time, floodlights hired and installed by Toby, and for ten days Venetia was busy rearranging and decorating the house with Sebastian, who was always ready to lend Mrs. Ball a hand in shifting furniture. Meanwhile George Ball cut the lawn, and trimmed and weeded the flower beds. The house rang with Sebastian and Venetia's laughter, and Toby was continually interrupting his work and coming to the door of his office to ask:

'What was that joke? Tell me what Sebastian said . . .' but his enquiries produced more merriment than explanations. Mother and son were always together, chattering eagerly, but losing no opportunity of teasing each other or of playing little practical jokes.

One afternoon Toby came into the kitchen where Venetia was polishing wine-glasses, and handed her a letter from Carlo which she immediately slipped into the pocket of her apron. Mrs. Ball and Sebastian could be heard breaking open a case of wine in the hall. Watching Venetia from the doorway, Toby thought of a northern landscape as the shadow of a cloud falls suddenly upon the hills. All that was smiling and happy had gone out of it, and her beauty had been left harsh, hungry, heart-rending.

He stood watching her silently for a few moments from the doorstep, then he lurched back into the kitchen and, taking the glass she was wiping and the cloth from her hand, he whispered:

'Go and read it.'

Venetia looked at him so humbly that he felt ashamed, and wondered why, and to what extent, it was his fault that she was unhappy and unsatisfied.

'And what can be done? How reconcile the irreconcilables? Impossible.'

Ten minutes later Venetia came back with a serene face and laid her arm on his shoulder and stroked his ear. Toby went back to his study, and soon afterwards heard her singing:

Oh Love, they wrong thee much
That say thy sweet is bitter,
When thy rich fruit is such
As nothing can be sweeter.
Fair house of joy and bliss
Where truest pleasure is,
I do adore thee;
I know thee what thou art
I serve thee with my heart,
And fall before thee.

But before Venetia had reached the end of the song, Toby had taken his rubber-shod stick and walked as quickly as he could manage to the edge of the Down to be out of earshot. There was a lark singing in the cloudless blue sky. Toby looked up at the bird until his eyes blurred and he could distinguish it no longer. The confounded bird was singing the same song as his wife—and he could not bear it. Then he sat down by the edge of the field of wheat which was beginning to turn greeny-gold. The lark stopped singing and Toby saw it drop among the corn.

'Death hath no fellow,' he said aloud, and getting on his feet, walked back to The Old Forge. He really must get off a letter to his Canadian correspondent.

Toby was in an uncontrollable state of agitation. Although he realized that he must appear calm and reasonable, that he must force himself to look at things from Venetia's point of view, the prospect of *his* coming to the party filled him with horror. It was his own doing. Venetia would never have thought of it, or if she had, would never have suggested it. But what did it matter? *His* coming only precipitated events which would have come about later inevitably. But no. The policy which he ought to pursue was to procrastinate: to put things off. Every week of separation would weaken Venetia's infatuation.

Moreover, was *he* the kind of man to remain chaste, or faithful for weeks on end? If *he* had not been invited to come south to this infernal party, *he* would have consoled himself with some girl in Manchester who was sentimental about sawdust. The obvious policy was to delay any meeting—instead of which he had hurried it forward. He had done so not really from generosity, but because in his extreme agitation he could not let the situation take its course. He had to talk to Venetia every ten minutes on some pretext or other. And as he could not confess his true feelings he had to make altruistic suggestions.

Toby was still in a state of extreme agitation, which amounted almost to agony of mind, when he walked into his study and picked up a sealed letter lying on his desk which had arrived during his short absence.

It was marked *Personal*, and contained a sealed inner envelope marked *Most Secret and Personal*. The letter ran as follows:

MOST SECRET   M.I.5.
(U.S. Ranking   W.O.
  Top Secret)

                 WHITEHALL, LONDON. S.W.1.

July

DEAR WING COMMANDER BARNARD,

               I am writing on a matter in which M.I.5 requires your co-operation. In the course of your business as Agent for a Dominion Government, you have access to material not necessarily on the Secret List, but which would be of value to a potential enemy of this country. M.I.5 has some evidence that your Secretary, Miss Angela Smith, is not a good security risk and has Communist affiliations. You are therefore forbidden to allow her access to any document which, in the National Interest, it is undesirable should be passed to foreign agents. At the same time you are required to do nothing which might awaken her suspicions.

While I feel sure that I can rely upon the full co-operation of an officer of your rank and antecedents, I must point out that any indiscretion on your part would terminate your usefulness to the Dominion Government in question.

            Yours sincerely,
               PERCY SWEETMAN-STREITFIELD.
               Captain.

Wing Commander T. Barnard,
               D.S.O., D.F.C., D.Sc., F.R.S.

On reading this communication, Toby's astonishment was only exceeded by his fury. His usual
patient, humorous expression, like that of a sea-lion
lending itself to the learning of a trick, was transformed into a really terrifying rage, and he seemed to
have grown much larger as he came smashing into the
room where Venetia and Sebastian were sitting. His
face was scarlet and his little moustache was bristling.

'I've got to get to the War House p.d.q. Can I
borrow your car?' he said to Venetia.

'What is it?' she asked.

'Some bloody lunatic making a bloody fool of himself . . . you may as well read it . . .' and Toby
threw the MOST SECRET letter on the table. 'A
damned little jumped-up . . .'

'When did you get it?' she asked.

'I found it on my table just this minute.'

'A dispatch rider handed a letter in to me half an
hour ago, and I put it on your desk,' said Sebastian.

'I never heard him,' said Venetia, puzzled.

'It was when you were singing.'

'I've got to go up at once and smash the blighter.
Either someone has been pulling his leg, or else it's
a conspiracy to try and put me out of business,' said
Toby a little more calmly.

'But is it so desperately urgent? Couldn't you
telephone?' asked Venetia.

Sebastian took the paper out of his mother's hands.

'Do you know the chap who wrote it?' he asked.

Toby was speaking, but he shook his head.

'I'll be back to-morrow afternoon at the latest. I shall go straight to the D. of I. . . .'

'Why don't you find out something about Captain Percy Sweetman-Streitfield before you go charging off?' Sebastian said with a curious intonation. Toby gave his son a quick glance. 'Not a bad idea. I'll ask Angela to look him up. Will you pack my bag, Venetia? Just pyjamas, toothbrush and shaving things. It will save time.'

Then, taking the letter, he went back to his study.

'You needn't bother about his bag,' said Sebastian as his mother was leaving the room. Then, as she turned to him, he burst into bubbling laughter.

'No, don't tell him. Let him find out for himself. I ought really to let him go to the D. of I.'

*   *   *

'When I get my hands on you I'll give you such a walloping,' said Toby, a quarter of an hour later.

'What's the matter now?' asked Sebastian innocently.

'Your officer is not in the Army list . . . to think that I should fall for a letter like that. No proper M.I.5 heading either. Making a monkey of your poor old dad. . . .'

Sebastian's practical joke delighted both his parents, and that evening the affection of all three overflowed. Toby opened a bottle of champagne and

Venetia and he drank 'To the health of the forger'.

Afterwards Toby explained that the reason why he was so easily taken in was that he was actually concerned with some very confidential documents. He was preparing a revenge on his son.

Angela had thrown herself with enthusiasm into the preparations for the party, and was continually ringing up from London to report on different kinds of biscuits and little sausages that she had discovered, and new dance records for the Hi-Fi. The day before the party, she came down bringing with her many parcels of smoked salmon, fruit and other perishables. She was lifting down the parcels from the railway carriage rack when, looking out of the window on to Newbury platform, she was astonished to see Venetia eagerly kissing a handsome swarthy stranger, who then put his free hand on her shoulder in a proprietary fashion, as they moved with oblivious happiness away from her window towards the ticket collector.

Angela was so astonished, so petrified that she scarcely remembered to get out herself. Then, with her face scarlet with anger and indignation, she told her porter to wait for a minute for the crowd to disperse. From the first moment, Angela was certain that this was the lover with whom Venetia was deceiving Toby, and whose existence she had discovered on her last visit to The Old Forge.

But that Venetia should choose to meet him on the

platform at Newbury and kiss him in a way that made their relationship obvious to dozens of people getting off or meeting the train, many of whom knew Toby and her by sight, this was abominable. It was obvious that she cared nothing about creating a scandal, or for Toby's feelings. Angela was still trembling with rage when three minutes later she came out into the station yard. There was, to her great relief, no sign of either Venetia, or of Toby. Her arrival had apparently been forgotten, so she took a taxi instead of ringing up Toby and asking him to meet her. If he had asked her how she came to miss Venetia, she could not have trusted herself to reply.

Directly after she reached The Old Forge, she handed Toby a dispatch case and, without even opening the precious parcels, told him that she had a bad headache, and went up to her room.

If she had seen the expression on the young man's face as he propelled Venetia towards the ticket collector, Angela would not have jumped to the conclusion that they were happy lovers.

'What is it?' asked Venetia.

'Let's get away and talk.'

'I was expecting to see Toby's secretary on this train. I think I ought to tell her to take a taxi, or to wait till I get back.'

'Let her rip. I've got something I want to say to you. Is this the family bus?'

Venetia slid into the driving seat of the old Lanchester saloon, drove quickly out of the station yard, and pulled up by the side of the road a little way past the race course.

'What is it?' she asked again, in a voice full of gentle tenderness.

'When you really wanted me, you brought your dinky two-seater. Now it's the family bus. And the family bus won't do.'

'Oh, darling. Please don't . . .'

'We planned to get three days together and I managed to work it. At the last minute the family makes demands on you, and you write to tell me that our holiday is washed out. You expect me to be pleased because your old man kindly allows me to come and entertain a party that he is throwing, and I am to be hidden away in some damned pub in the hopes of seeing you for the middle of the afternoon. I don't think it's good enough.'

'But, darling, I explained, or tried to explain about the polio.'

'I'm not the type to be jealous of a kid. If he was ill, or if you were really worried about him, I wouldn't say a word. But you've scrapped our holiday just because you don't want the kid to know that I'm on the map. He's got to know it—and pronto. 'Cause I'm going to take you back with me to Manchester.'

'Darling, you make it so impossibly difficult.'

Venetia took Carlo's head in her hands and kissed

him. Then she drove on to a lonely place where
Carlo's jealousy was temporarily quieted. But it was
almost time for dinner when she got back to The
Old Forge, after dropping Carlo at his hotel, and she
could not think what explanation to give to Sebastian,
or to Angela. An accident would have to do.

' A puncture and the spare wheel was flat,' she said
in reply to Sebastian's question.

To her surprise, Toby came to help her out.

'That's entirely my fault. I've known it was flat
and kept meaning to have it blown up. But it's so
out of the way, and I've been in a hurry. I suppose
you waited to get the puncture mended.'

'Yes. . . . And then I had the wheel put back
again. That was right, I suppose?'

'Splendid. Much better to wait and get the job
properly done. We can't afford to have the car un-
serviceable to-morrow. By the way, Angela arrived
here with a bad headache and has gone off to bed. I
put my head in and she said she had taken a codeine
and a sleeping pill, and would rather not be
disturbed.'

After supper, Venetia and Sebastian unpacked the
parcels which Angela had brought and put the
smoked salmon and the fresh caviare in the
refrigerator.

'We had better all go to bed early,' said Venetia.

Toby went with her to the bottom of the stairs,
then he went back into the dining-room, opened

the dispatch case and began sorting through the papers.

'What are all those about?' asked Sebastian.

Toby looked up at his son and said with a perfectly straight face: 'Don't mention it to anyone—not even to your mother. Angela brought down some absolutely top-secret plans, which some people would stick at nothing to get hold of. It is conceivable that an attempt may be made to steal them under cover of this party. I want you to keep an eye open for any possible gate-crasher.'

'Gosh! What a thrill!' exclaimed Sebastian.

Venetia was still awake when Toby went into the bedroom.

'Oh, darling. I'm so grateful to you. I don't know what I should do without you.'

'Don't bother to tell me about it now. I can see you are most frightfully tired. Tell me some other time, if you want to.'

Venetia nodded her head and said nothing, but when he had joined her in bed, she kissed him several times. Toby, who had taken some pills because his leg was hurting him, went to sleep at once, but Venetia lay awake for an hour, wondering. What would Carlo be like? She was to take him out to lunch next day.

Venetia was not feeling in the mood for physical love on the high Downs, or in the woods near Silchester and, after picking up Carlo, drove to the river,

94

where she hired a punt. She was at home in small boats, and it had not occurred to her that, if Carlo were not, he might resent her superiority. He had always accepted without question that she should drive her own car, but that was because he was able to drive well himself.

But instead of reclining peacefully on the cushions and enjoying the grace with which she handled the punt pole, he chose to sulk and said little until they had disembarked for lunch on the shaven lawn of a riverside inn.

It was a lovely day. The sun was hot; the reflections of the willows, and of the old bridge beyond, were broken only by the movements of two swans pressing on the water as they quested for bits of bread, and it seemed ridiculous that Carlo should continue out of temper. But Venetia said nothing.

'Any woman can make a monkey of me,' he said at last. 'I'm like that. I never say no. Why should I? I'm no Joseph. Life's easier if you take it that way. We show people don't stay long enough in one place to lose our sleep over women. They can't all follow me around like you've done.'

Venetia laughed, but said nothing, and after a pause Carlo continued: 'Women were a piece of pie for little Carlo till he married a girl in the circus. After that, did I have to watch my step, or did I? I guess Miranda is the Spanish for green eyes.' Then as Venetia still was silent, looking at him with a mock-

95

ing, amused smile, he pulled an envelope out of his pocket.

'I've brought some photos along for you to see. That's Miranda in tights and a bra.'

The photograph, which had obviously been taken for publicity, was of a lovely young girl holding out her arms in invitation while she revealed a perfect set of teeth in an enormous smile. As Venetia said nothing, Carlo handed her a number of action photographs taken by flashlight, of Miranda on the trapeze. The muscles were taut, the body exquisitely graceful, but there was a concentrated, embittered expression on the young features.

'Goodness! What a lovely creature! You never told me that she was so perfect and so proud and so aloof. I do wish I could get to know her. I should love to meet her,' exclaimed Venetia with genuine enthusiasm. It was not what Carlo had wanted, or expected. He stared at her astonished.

'The answer is a raspberry. You scare me pink. Miranda'd carve you into cats' meat if she knew about us.'

'Isn't is just possible that she may have found someone who suits her better than you do in Sweden? In which case I don't suppose she would be as jealous as you like to imagine,' said Venetia.

'Miranda knows that if I ever found her playing about with another man I should tie her up and give her the thrashing of her life,' said Carlo venomously.

Venetia stared at him, scarcely able to believe that he had actually said what she had heard him say. For a few moments surprise prevented her from feeling indignation. Then, as she felt herself growing hot with anger, she asked: 'Is that what you believe Toby ought to do with me?'

Carlo grinned.

'No. He's not so dumb as to try. He knows that in your marriage you are tops and that you'd walk out on him if he did. But if you were married to me would I take a slipper to you. . . . Oh, Boy! . . . Would I not?'

Venetia was so furious that she was silent, and Carlo continued: 'I bet it would make you very loving, so that sometimes you would be asking for it.'

There was a long silence.

'You didn't succeed in making me feel jealous, but you have certainly made me feel surprise,' said Venetia quietly.

'Always a hundred per cent on the level,' said Carlo. His mood had changed and he was in high glee the whole of the return journey. But, as she punted, Venetia was very conscious that 'a hundred per cent on the level' was just what she was not. She was very glad to have the current with her, shortening the time that Carlo and she would be together.

7

ANGELA had been astonished to see Venetia get into her little car and drive away in the middle of the morning. She succeeded, however, in stifling her indignation, but a little later said to Toby:

'Do you know when Venetia is coming back? Mrs. Ball will want directions and I shall be sure to make mistakes and do things that Venetia wouldn't like.'

'What sort of things?' asked Toby.

'Well, there are the flowers to arrange,' replied Angela.

'Don't worry. Everything is laid on and there won't be any difficulties. Venetia will be back some time after lunch, which leaves plenty of time for her to do the flowers herself.'

'I never admire you more, Toby, than at moments like these. You are the only man I know who always takes things calmly and doesn't fuss in a crisis of this sort . . .'

'Crisis?' interposed Toby, rather dryly.

'I mean Venetia's going off so unaccountably.'

'I never try to account for Venetia's actions. I

know there is a satisfactory reason for them: a reason which is valid for her at all events.'

'I think you are the most extraordinary man: there is no one in the world like you. I wish we were all as calm and loyal, but I'm afraid we all, that is —Venetia and I—both trade on it . . .'

Toby interrupted her with:

'It's very, very sweet of you to pay me all these compliments. There's really no occasion for them.' And he patted her on the shoulder and kissed her lightly on the top of her head, though he would have liked to have said: 'For Christ's sake shut up, you impertinent little bitch.' Fortunately Angela could not see his expression, as he gave her the kiss.

'Toby, you are a darling,' she exclaimed.

'Well, in that case you won't mind taking down the following letter, which I shall forget if I leave it till to-morrow, when we shall both have most frightful hangovers.'

And, before she could reply, he began dictating.

For the moment he had disposed of Angela.

There was, however, an awkward constraint at lunch, as Sebastian was more astonished at his mother's absence than Angela, and loudly maintained his dissatisfaction until Toby was forced to say:

'You had better have it out with her herself. But don't you think it's just possible that she has a surprise in store for all of us?'

When lunch was over, Toby went upstairs and lay down on the bed to rest his leg. The evening would be tiring, but the idea of resting was bad, for directly he was alone he began thinking that Venetia was in the arms of a man who was taking his pleasure of her, and that he would have to meet and speak to him that evening in the presence of nearly a hundred people. Carlo would smile—and what would he not read into that smile? Carlo and Venetia would dance together all the evening: the women watching would make comments; they would say: 'They are made for each other.' And what would he not read into such words?

Toby knew that, when the moment arrived, he could trust his self-control—he knew that whatever happened he would behave with dignity. He knew also that as regards himself he did not really care a damn if scandal were being talked, or if he was contemptuously regarded as a *mari complaisant*. What mattered was Venetia's happiness, and that she might, without guessing it until too late, be going to ruin her life. Everything else, even the emotional shock that the knowledge of the affair would give Sebastian, was petty. But lying alone on the bed where Venetia and he had slept together for so many years, he could not bear it. He could not continue to control his emotions. It was obvious to him that Venetia and he were bound to make each other so unhappy that parting was the only solution.

Separation would be easy and desirable for Venetia
—but for him? Toby saw clearly that for him there
would be nothing left in life. What about Sebastian?
The boy was old enough to stand on his own feet.
It would be a shock to him and he might suffer a good
deal, but he was young and resilient enough to get
over it. The more he thought about it, the clearer
it became to Toby that Venetia must be set free. She
could not be tied by the feelings of a boy of Sebastian's age. She could not be tied to a man she was
not in love with. Perhaps he had better find out
whether the job in India, or another one like it, was
not still open to him. Venetia would need all the
money he could give her. He couldn't run the risk
of her being dependent on Carlo. India, at all
events, would be highly paid. And Toby suddenly
saw himself as he would be in three or four years
time—oozing whisky, self-pity and embarrassing
confidences about his married life, cursing the native
servants, the edge of his brain gone so that he was
incapable of doing, or caring about his job. Suicide
would be better than that. Such a clean and sharp
decision would be a relief. But suicide was a luxury
which he could not afford: he must continue to be
earning money; he must be there to help Venetia if
she needed it, and to keep an eye on Sebastian.

Toby had lain on the bed with his face buried in
the pillow and his shoulders shaking, not with tears
but with a nervous twitch which he could not be

bothered to control, when the door was softly opened, and Venetia came in. She was much earlier than he had expected, and he did not know that she was there until she asked gently:

'What is the matter, my dear?'

Toby lifted his big head, and she saw that his cheeks were flushed and that his eyes were red.

'Tell me, what are you feeling?' she asked, sitting down on the edge of the bed and putting her hand on his shoulder.

'My feelings are despicable. Don't let's go into them. But tell me what you are feeling and thinking. You are early.'

'I don't want to tell you what I am feeling,' replied Venetia, taking his hand and holding it tightly. Toby took this to mean that she had reached the limit of endurance and wanted to go away with Carlo at once. Perhaps she had already promised to do so.

'I shall find it much easier to get through this evening if you tell me the worst. Not knowing for certain is torture. Do speak.'

There was a long silence and Venetia sat with her brow furrowed, still clinging tightly to Toby's hand. At last, turning her eyes away from his, she said in little more than a whisper:

'I don't think I'm really very much in love with Carlo.'

At her words Toby suddenly felt so tired and so

unreal, that he found it difficult to speak, and it was almost mechanically that he said:

'Oh, my darling, I do feel the most intense pity for you. I have been longing for this to come. . . . I never thought it would. I'll do anything I can to help . . . to make it easier for you.'

'I can't promise that I shan't fall in love with someone else that you'll dislike even more.'

For a split second Toby reflected that, even at that moment, the cat had to play with the wretched mouse.

'Does he guess that your feelings have changed?'

Venetia shook her head.

'I don't think he's really in love with me—only with what he would like me to be and that he imagines is me.'

'Perhaps that was true of you also—and that you really are more in love with love than with Carlo.' Toby found that he could say Carlo's name. For weeks he had not been able to say 'Carlo' when he spoke to Venetia. It had always been 'he'.

He got off the bed and shook himself. He wanted to cry and to get drunk. 'Probably I shall do both,' he said to himself, then aloud: 'Now for the party!' though there were several hours to wait.

And off he went to discuss with Sebastian and Mr. Ball the best way of parking the visitors' cars round the gravel sweep in front of the house.

When Venetia followed him downstairs she came

face to face with Angela, who struck her immediately as looking very odd. While at work she was always sleek and efficient and, in the hours of relaxation, gay and uninhibited, but at that moment her face was swollen and flushed with emotion and her person fluffed up, reminding Venetia of an indignant, broody hen.

'I must speak to you in private: somewhere where we shan't be overheard, or interrupted,' she said, gazing at Venetia with a steadfast glare.

'Come upstairs to my bedroom,' said Venetia, and turning she led the way.

'What's the matter?' she asked, locking the door and noticing that Angela was carrying the bag which she remembered choosing as Toby's Christmas present for the girl.

Angela stood glaring at her in silence with such obvious hostility that Venetia managed to control her impatience and to wonder what kind of unpleasantness was coming.

'Is it anything to do with the party?'

'No. It's a personal matter.'

Angela opened the bag, took out a letter and handed it to her. There was no envelope and it was in Carlo's handwriting.

'I found it lying on the floor in the cloak-room,' said Angela portentously, and then suddenly a rush of words followed.

'I read the first few lines . . . they contain filthy,

obscene words . . . that no decent woman would allow anyone to write to her, or utter in her presence. . . . You needn't think I'm strait-laced. I don't mind filthy words in a joke, or men swearing . . .'

Venetia unfolded the letter and read the first sentence. Then she said rather pedantically:

'Those words are what love is about. If you don't know that, you know nothing.' She felt surprised and relieved to discover that in this astounding interview she was keeping her temper and could feel coldly detached. 'You may quite well object to them as a matter of taste,' she added, 'but they were not written for you to read.'

'I am going to be quite open,' said Angela. 'I think you are a degenerate and a nymphomaniac. I have known for some time that you have been deceiving Toby and have been unfaithful to him. This letter shows you are unworthy of any consideration. I care for him deeply. I know that I can make him infinitely happier than you have ever been able to . . . I don't want to reproach you, but to ask you to release him. If it is a question of money, I know, and you know too, that Toby will be most generous to you. . . . The only thing you can decently do is to give Toby material for a divorce. You don't have to manufacture it either, because I've got it. I can tell you that. That letter is sufficient. If I had handed it to Toby he would have divorced you. I am giving it to you because it is too disgusting, and it would have upset him too much. But it's not the only evidence.'

'Toby doesn't want to divorce me,' said Venetia.

The two women looked at each other in silence, Angela with a glare of dogged determination and flushed with indignation, Venetia with ironical contempt and a touch of pity. Finally she said:

'I shall be very grateful if you will mind your own business until Toby takes you into his confidence— and please stop reading my letters.'

'I picked it up in the cloak-room, where it was lying on the floor, and I only read the first and last lines,' said Angela, flushing still more with anger because she had allowed herself to be put on the defensive when she was properly the accuser. And now she was being made to tell a lie—though only in Toby's interests.

'I suppose it must have fallen out of the pocket of my coat,' said Venetia. 'It's really rather lucky that you picked it up and not Sebastian or Mrs. Ball. I care more about their feelings than about yours. If Toby had read it, he would not have been shocked by the words you object to.'

She unlocked the door, and, as Angela stood silent, showing no disposition to move, she added impatiently:

'You've said all that you wanted to, haven't you?'

'Aren't you going to give Toby up? Have I got to make you?' whispered Angela.

'I'm certainly not going to give him up, as you call it. You are living in a world of illusions which can only make you desperately unhappy. So I must tell you that I know for a fact that Toby is not in the least bit in love with you, and that there is no chance of his ever becoming so. I expect he is looking for you now. Do, for goodness sake, go away.'

Angela went out without a word.

'. . . the girl,' Venetia exclaimed, using one of the words that had so shocked Angela in Carlo's letter. Remembering that the girl was not shocked by its use in swearing, Venetia laughed slightly hysterically.

'What an overture to our party! And, my God, what a day! First Carlo behaves like the selfish pig he turns out to be. Then I'm weak enough to tell Toby what I'm feeling, and then Angela goes batty. I must have an hour's rest.'

8

'You are looking very lovely, as you always do,' said Toby, going into the bedroom after tying his black bow. Venetia had put on a dress of heavy, black watered silk, cut very low, strapless, and very tight about the waist, with voluminous skirts which sprang out almost like a crinoline. She handed him a ruby and pearl necklace set in gold. He fastened it for her, and as he took his hands from the clasp, she turned swiftly towards him, put her hands round his neck and kissed him. The touch of his white, wiry moustache pleased her, as always.

'What a moment to try to inflame my passions!' he growled. 'Look—you've covered my coat with face powder.'

'You aren't very grateful, you old bear.'

'I don't want to influence you in making your decision,' said Toby, suddenly changing the whole tone of their remarks. 'But there is one thing I implore you. Make up your mind whether you are in love, or whether you are not. And when you have done so, *act*. The cruellest thing you can do is to play cat and mouse with him.'

'You must let me do things in my own way.'

Toby touched her on the shoulder affectionately. His touch meant 'I have said what I was going to say, and am not going to add to it at present.' Venetia recognized the message and moved towards the door.

'Her own way,' reflected Toby, 'is probably the way of the cat with the mouse. But conceivably all may come right in the end.'

The bell rang announcing the first arrival, as he followed her downstairs.

As happens at almost every party, two or three pairs of the least socially gifted guests arrived early. As they were welcomed, as they were helped out of their coats, as they were given drinks, they plunged Toby and Venetia into the deep freeze of despair. After listening to the mumbled commonplaces, they became so numbed that they could barely articulate a wooden welcome to the next arrivals. An interminable five minutes followed, during which one or two of their unlucky guests began to wonder whether it would not be better to go away and return later.

Then came a great rush, mostly from the further side of Wiltshire: gay creatures who had come to enjoy themselves, or had brought pleasure with them. As many of them knew each other intimately, they brushed aside their frozen, feeble hosts and, by so doing, infused them with a little hope. It occurred to both Venetia and to Toby that the party might be quite a success without them. And in the guise of showing a small group of guests the garden, they slipped away, leaving Sebastian to greet the later arrivals.

'I'm Carlo—Carlo Marx. I guess you're Sebastian?' said one of these, as he unwound a white silk muffler and slipped out of his elegant black overcoat.

Sebastian was astonished by him. In the first place, Carlo was the only man wearing a white tie and tails, and his immaculate clothes and his glossy black head, with every curl in place, was in marked contrast to the Wiltshire nobility and gentry. Young Lord Inkpen, for example, who had immediately preceded Carlo, was wearing green corduroy trousers and a plum-coloured pullover, and he had obviously not visited a barber's shop for several weeks. In the second place, Sebastian thought that the name Karl Marx must be an assumed one—possibly the fellow, using the technique of the double bluff, was a cunningly disguised Communist—and, in the third place, the glossy visitor knew his name and kept looking at him with keen curiosity. All this made Sebastian wonder if Carlo had not come to spy out the land before trying to burgle the house and steal the top secret drawings which Toby had mentioned the previous evening.

As his parents had vanished, Sebastian, after giving Carlo a drink, went up to Angela, who was visible through the door of the drawing-room, and asked her:

'Do you know who the chap in tails is? He calls himself Karl Marx.'

The question took Angela completely by surprise. She had never imagined that Venetia would dare to invite her lover to Toby's party. For a moment she looked stunned. Then she replied:

'He's an admirer of your mother's.'

'An admirer? I have never heard her talk about him,' said Sebastian slowly. 'Are you quite sure he's not a business friend of Toby's?'

'I know that he isn't. I don't think Toby has ever met him.'

Sebastian went back to his duties of carrying round a tray of sherry and cocktails, determined to keep a sharp watch on Carlo for the rest of the evening. Thus he was watching when, a minute later, Venetia came in, and he noticed a propitiatory look on his mother's face as she greeted Carlo. Then he saw her turn to Toby and heard her say:

'This is Carlo, Toby. This is my husband.'

He saw his father stiffen and stand up a little straighter before he spoke, saying:

'It's most awfully good of you to come.'

And Sebastian knew that, even if Toby had never met him before, he knew who he was and felt uncomfortable with him.

Later, when the big drawing-room was cleared and dancing started, he saw Carlo dancing with his mother, and then in an interval, while the others watched, they danced first a tango and then a rumba. There was prolonged applause after each dance.

Sebastian went up to his mother when it was over and asked for the next dance—a waltz. While they were dancing, he asked her with affected innocence:

'Who is your wonderful partner, Mr. Marx?'

'He's a splendid dancer, as you have seen.'

'He's absolutely marvellous—and so, of course, are you,' said Sebastian. 'How long have you known him? Where does he spring from and where is he staying?'

'Not very long really. He works in a circus, and he is staying at the Rose and Crown.' Venetia had forgotten Sebastian's anger when she had told him and Toby about being taken into the tigers' cage, but Sebastian had not, and his suspicions of Carlo were reinforced by those of jealousy.

'Oh, how marvellous! How absolutely delightful!' exclaimed a woman's voice which filled the room. It was Lady Ida Benskin who had arrived very late.

'I've been pining to see you, Mr. Marx! After that little party of mine I chased miles and miles over the whole of England asking everyone I met if they had seen any tigers! And they all seemed to think that I was quite mad. It was so disappointing, and all your fault because you never put your address on the letter you wrote after the party!'

After acknowledging Carlo's salutation, Lady Ida turned to her host and hostess.

'How brilliantly clever of you, darling Venetia, to

keep in touch with dear Carlo. But I dare say it's he who keeps in touch with you! You are certainly looking very lovely. I must see you dance the tango together.'

'You came just too late to see us,' said Venetia.

'Well, you must dance again, and then Carlo must tell us one of his perfectly divine stories. You remember the one about the midget, Mr. Barnard? I always feel so desperately sorry for freaks and cripples. You will back me up in insisting on a story, won't you?'

'Go and persuade him. I'm sure you can, if any-one,' said Toby. 'But excuse me now, I've got to make the punch.' And he walked away. Venetia followed him a moment afterwards.

'I should like to strangle that woman,' she said when they were alone together in the kitchen. Toby was laughing.

'Nothing matters, darling, if you're still fond of me,' he said.

'Carlo's in a filthy mood,' said Venetia. She turned and went back to her guests.

'Well, hurrah for that. The filthier his mood, the happier is mine,' said Toby, but she had already left the room.

The punch was made and Toby went back on to the floodlit lawn. It was time to shepherd the people indoors, time for Carlo's story, which should make a diversion and encourage everyone to stay on.

'Do I want them to stay on?' he asked himself, and then: 'What sort of a story will Carlo tell? Well, I am not responsible. It's up to him.' The young man, looking, Toby admitted to himself, overwhelmingly handsome in his white waistcoat and tails, was standing beside Josiah Fancourt, who was wearing a cream-coloured tropical dinner jacket which had been made for him when he had gone on a cruise to the West Indies five years before. It smelt of mothballs, and the red-faced old fellow was indulging in some rather tropical reminiscences, about coloured girls swimming out to meet the ship.

'My dear Marx, I want everyone to come indoors and drink hot punch. Lady Ida says that you are going to tell us a story,' said Toby.

'Pleased to oblige, in any way, I'm sure,' said Carlo showing his perfect teeth.

Sebastian was the shepherd's dog and, urged by him, stray couples were rounded up and the company obediently trooped indoors. There were delighted exclamations from *décolletées* ladies on seeing the big fire blazing in the hearth; punch was distributed and accepted, and at last, when the company was settled, Toby said:

'Allow me to introduce, to those who have not already met or danced with him, Mr. Carlo Marx, a brilliant psychologist who works in a circus. Lady Ida has persuaded Mr. Marx to tell us a story.' And Toby retreated to a seat near the door.

Angela was in a corner feeding Lord Inkpen on marrons glacés; hearing Toby's words, she looked up astounded.

At the last minute Venetia came into the room and made her way quickly towards Toby, and then sat down on a stool at his feet. Carlo pushed his chair forward so that the light fell on his lean profile crowned with glistening black curls. He was looking aggressively handsome, and far more sure of himself than she had ever seen him.

'Here is a little parable about a child's innocence and how it can keep people living together who really hate each other,' he began. At these words Venetia half-turned to Toby and, taking his hand, gave it a squeeze, almost digging her nails in it. Toby realized that it was a warning, and pressed her shoulder with his knee.

'I am afraid many of you will think my story cynical and unpleasant: however it is true.

'Pyramids are built up from the ground, and everything depends on the solidity of the base. In a human pyramid this is a strong man, and the base of the one I am going to tell you about was an Italian called Leonidas. As a boy he had started on the flying trapeze. But he grew too big and put on weight, and by the time he was thirty-two, when I met him first, he was six foot three and weighed seventeen stone. All the same he'd got where he wanted: he'd built up a human pyramid which was

116

also a trapeze act. He started fifteen feet above the ground, standing on an outsize trapeze: the bar was a foot wide, and it hung down across the middle of the ring on steel cables.'

Carlo paused. Up till that moment he had spoken in a tired voice as though he were repeating something that he had memorized. Then he suddenly seemed to interrupt himself and speak extempore: 'I tell you: it was rather like those cradles that workmen use for painting the outside of a building.' The changed voice and the image helped. Attention had been captured.

'The actual pyramid was Leonidas as the base with a Neapolitan called Salvatore standing on his shoulders, a Sicilian girl called Anna on Salvatore with a child called Eugenia, who was Leonidas's daughter by his first wife, standing on her shoulders. Two other girls, one of whom was my wife, were placed fan-like on each side. They hung inwards, head down, at an angle of forty-five with their feet about a yard apart, held in loops on the steel cable, gripping a garter on Salvatore's knee with one hand and a loop of leather harness on Leonidas's shoulder with the other. Though they looked as though Leonidas was supporting them, they added nothing to the weight, and gave a good deal of lateral stiffness. When they were all in place, assistants started the trapeze swinging to and fro. Anna and the little girl had to keep their balance by the usual trapezist technique of leaning over as the swing gathered speed, and then letting the trapeze catch up with them, as it slowed down to a standstill, first forwards and then rhythmically backwards. It looked harder and more difficult than it was. The act ended with the two side girls letting go with their hands, and each catching her own small side trapeze swinging in from each side towards the big one. As each caught her bar she disengaged her feet out of the loops. When they were settled and in position the child dived forward and her hands were caught by the girl in front, and Anna did a back somersault, and was caught by the other girl. Salvatore bent down, took hold of Leonidas's hands and did a handspring. Leonidas kept him balanced, while the net was removed and the big trapeze lowered to the ground. It was quite a skilful turn, but it is the people I want to tell you about—not the act.

'I got to know them well when my wife took on the job of being the wing trapeze girl, responsible for catching Eugenia at the break-up. Leonidas was a big simpleton. If anything worried him he used to come round in the evening to my caravan and spill it all to my wife and me. Not that Miranda could stand having him around.

'"That fat ox," she used to say. What she hated about him was his lack of pride. No Spaniard would ever have spilled it all, like this man from North Italy. He came, by the way, from Murano in the

Italian Tyrol, and, of course, Leonidas was just a stage name.

'Not being Spanish, I thought he was a good average, only a bit simple. "It's on my conscience," he used to say, "that Anna and Eugenia don't feel about the act the way I do." Then he'd shut his eyes and give a long sigh. "Maybe I ought not to put it first. Maybe I ought to send Eugenia to a convent school. She is innocent. She doesn't know what evil there is . . ." Sigh again like he were ill, and hadn't long to live.

'"And Anna! She is a sweet, pure girl. I married her so my poor child should have a mother. I keep thinking that, now she's married, she'd be happier in the home." Miranda and I had seen as soon as we laid eyes on her that Anna was as hard-boiled as they come, but we couldn't say so—and old Leonidas would sigh again and say: "I would give her anything. . . . But maybe my act is unique, and how could I earn a living if I broke it up? A strong man act would never make the dough like a pyramid. It would be finish for me. . . . Just go in a sideshow."

'If anything went wrong with Leonidas and his pyramid, it would have been a big loss for the circus. So I used to lay it on as thick as I dared—tell him he was a noble character, and that his scruples did him credit. Then Miranda would tell him that the child's innocence was safer with her father watching over her. There was plenty wickedness among the girls

119

in convent schools. And that Anna was proud of being such a swell acrobat and married to a strong man.

' "I'd do anything on earth to make that woman happy," and Leonidas would sigh, as though he wasn't a newly married man making big money. "I wouldn't mind how much I were to suffer."

' "Nobody is asking you to suffer," I would say, feeling fed-up. I didn't guess how soon his sentiments would be tested. It was quite true that Anna worshipped the little girl. And so did Salvatore. It was like a cult. And the craziest of the three was Salvatore—he wasn't related to her. But you know what Italians are like about children. Anna was a piece of cheesecake, only about eighteen years old—smashing figure, but, except for her feelings for the child, she was a selfish little bitch. She had thought it smart to marry the boss—but very soon Leonidas gave her the willies. I guess it was his softness and his way of sighing. It amused her to excite Salvatore, and she kept on at him until, one day, she went too far. . . . Then out of pure devilment, she told her husband what had happened. I expect she wanted to see what he'd do about it. It's what ninety-nine women in a hundred do, anyway. Well, this blew up just as we had finished rehearsing, before we opened in London for the Christmas season. I think old Leonidas would have broken his contract and liquidated his pyramid, if it hadn't been for the child. Instead of giving Anna a hiding and finding a new man to take Salvatore's place, he got them together and made them swear not to let Eugenia know anything about it. The child's innocence was all that mattered. And they both felt just the same way. So Anna went on living with her husband, only going out after midnight to misconduct herself with Salvatore when Eugenia was asleep, and then going back to Leonidas in the van in the early hours. Of course she slept with him too.'

Carlo paused and looked about him. His audience was clearly uncomfortable and felt that there was something unpleasant behind the tale, which was unpleasant enough in itself. One or two cleared their throats, and offered each other drinks. But the story was not over, and Carlo went on with an unpleasant edgy note in his rather grating, clipped cockney.

'It must have been a bit trying for them: twice a day all three were in close contact wearing nothing but tights and a jock strap, and twice a day Salvatore's life was in Leonidas's hands. He could have knocked him off in full sight of the audience with no one being able to prove that it wasn't an accident. But Salvatore thought he was safe, and amused himself making the big fellow chew the rag.

'One day when he had been a little clumsy at the finish, Salvatore said to him in front of us all:

'"If only you grew horns that I could hold on to, I could do a much better handspring." The child

Eugenia clapped her hands and thought it a wonderful idea. Then, when she was out of earshot, Salvatore said: "I can't think why you haven't grown them: I'm damned if I don't do my best." Anna laughed when he said that, and her husband looked at her like he was puzzled. He was too dumb to see that she was finished with him. You might have thought it would be comical to see a strong man, who could have strangled Anna with one hand, and Salvatore with the other, being made a fool of in public. It wasn't funny. It just made one want to go in a corner and spew.

'Miranda kept saying to me: "Why doesn't someone tell that ox to give Anna a beating-up?" I had to make her keep her mouth shut.

'The pyramid was a big draw, and did we keep our traps shut when that kid was around? I guess we walked on eggs. She never spotted a thing, and the act lasted out the London season.

'Almost directly afterwards the kid caught the measles, and her illness linked 'em all up together again. For Eugenia nearly went home, and when she was at her worst all three confessed their sins to a priest and asked to be forgiven. I don't know how long they stayed repentant. When I last heard of them, Leonidas's pyramid was going strong with the same cast, except my wife, who had left because she felt the way Spaniards do about the Wops. She got a far better job as the star, in a really big trapeze act.'

Carlo stopped speaking, his story was apparently finished.

'What was the child like?' Sebastian asked unexpectedly.

'Most ordinary-looking, with sandy hair and red rims to her eyes. A dreamy kid and a bit dumb like her father. But after a while, I saw that I had been pretty nearly as dumb as Eugenia. Watching them every night made me see things: I started seeing pyramids all around. They are real enough. Where-ever I go now, I find myself right among them. The fat old husband usually keeps base—not always—for the lover can be the strong man and the husband the light-weight. Usually the lover reckons he's getting the best of it—though my hunch is that the wife, with her pretty curves and sharp tongue, gets the right end. Then there's whatever holds the pyramid together. If there's a kid you can bet the sweet little innocent ch-hild is the Duro-fix. Sometimes the wife and the boy-friend can't stand on their own feet, and so they have to be carried. Sometimes it's the husband's incredible generosity of heart that keeps the three of them gummed up—other times it's their self-sacrifice and generosity to him—to save his respectability, or his job. Any tale will do. If the wife has a headache once a month it needs two men to take care of it. Whatever it is supposed to be, it makes me tired, for it's one big lie.

'The pyramid sticks together because it has to do

its act. The three of them are pros, and owe it to their public.

'I didn't know that when I first started watching Leonidas, Anne and Salvatore with little Eugenia on top.. Every time they went on, I was waiting for a blow-up that never came.

'But it did one big thing for me: it taught me that this boy Carlo will never play in pyramids. I would rather swallow swords in a sideshow, or train performing fleas.'

During the last part of Carlo's story apprehensive glances had been exchanged, knuckles had whitened, and eyes grown stony. His audience felt itself insulted, and the sense of scandalized outrage was sufficient to prevent smiles being exchanged, or eyebrows raised at the expense of host and hostess. Carlo had put himself so far outside the pale that his audience felt that no inferences should be made from anything he said or did. For the time being, the upper class of Wiltshire had closed its ranks in unexpected solidarity.

As Carlo finished, there was a stir and movement, several men saying simultaneously: 'Wouldn't you like to come into the garden? . . . stretch your legs . . . a bit cramped . . . awfully hot fire for summer.' One or two women began to say that perhaps they ought to be going, and then silently realized that it might seem marked to run away at the first moment.

There were no comments on the story, and no one

thanked Carlo, or went up to him. In the first hub-bub of movement and conversation, Venetia swiftly left the room with her face very pale. She was taken completely by surprise by Carlo's behaviour, and felt so furious that she could not trust herself to speak.

Carlo, finding himself left alone, went up to Toby and asked: 'Have you any comments, sir?'

'I think it was extremely lucky for them that they were all Roman Catholics, so that a priest could recon-cile them,' said Toby with great geniality. Then, as it appeared that Carlo was going to say something else to him, he continued: 'The last part was very illuminating, but I don't think it went down well with your listeners.'

'I would worry,' said Carlo, but it was obvious that he was slightly taken aback.

A few couples began dancing again, but neither Venetia nor Carlo took any part in it. Carlo went up to the sideboard and began drinking steadily. An hour later, when the party had thinned out consider-ably, he found Venetia in the next room and said rather thickly: 'Not going to go without you come too. Go get your coat.' She looked at him, and seeing that he was more than a little drunk, nodded her head and went out of the room. In the garden she found Molly Bisset, the eighteen-year-old daughter of the racing trainer. She had been cap-tured by Josiah Fancourt, who was telling her his tropical stories.

'Will you do me a signal service, Molly?' she asked. 'It's to take Carlo, who told that story, back to the Rose and Crown where he is staying. He hasn't a car, and is insisting that I should take him. He isn't really very high . . . only bloody-minded about me.'

Josiah, who had overheard what she said, chuckled, and Venetia turned to him and said:

'I'll give you his coat, Josiah, and you can help him into it.'

'You know I'd always do anything you ever asked me, Venetia. I think that you are the most beautiful woman that I know. I've never dared tell you before . . . I love you . . . everyone else does too . . . unfortunately for me,' said Molly, and she went off to find her duffle coat.

Then she walked up to Carlo and introduced herself.

'I'm Molly Bisset. I've volunteered to drive you back to the Rose and Crown.'

'I'm waiting for Venetia, actually,' he replied.

'I think we'll find her in the hall saying good-bye to people,' said Molly.

In the hall Josiah was waiting with Carlo's coat and helped him into it.

'Good-bye, Toby: good-bye, Venetia. I'm kidnapping Carlo,' cried Molly, gaily pushing him in front of her out of the door. He offered no resistance.

9

THE party was over too late for any post-mortem discussion of it, and Angela went to her room but did not sleep—did not want to sleep. She felt that she was going mad, but that before she began to rave and gibber she must expose Venetia—at whatever cost—to Toby or Sebastian. Such wickedness could not be allowed to go unpunished.

How could Venetia have had the audacity to invite Carlo to the party? How could she have had the vile hypocrisy to sit holding Toby's hand while the partner of her lust told that disgusting, insulting story?

'I will expose her to-morrow. I shall be ruthless. I will make it impossible for Toby to turn a blind eye—I will show them to him in each other's arms . . . when everything is purulent and septic, I must cut it open, if Toby is to recover. . . .'

Dawn came and Angela lay wide awake, laying her plans like an avenging angel. She would have given a great deal for a cup of coffee, but she would not get up for breakfast as she could not face sitting down at the same table as her victims—innocent or guilty.

Sebastian slept late and only appeared for lunch, but at half-past eight Venetia woke to find Toby propped up beside her, reading *The Darling Buds of May*.

'I have made up my mind to go and see Carlo first thing this morning and tell him that it is all over,' she said.

'Make quite sure why you are doing this. It must only be because you want to. Not for my sake, or Sebastian's. If you do it for him or me you will destroy whatever relationship still exists,' said Toby.

'You sound horribly theoretical, as though you were reading aloud from a text-book,' said Venetia.

'I dare say I do. But, if so, the text-book is right and says what I feel most strongly. If you make sacrifices, you will ruin everything—my life just as much as your own.'

'No, it's not really for your sake or for his. I'm not in love with Carlo. I think that in spite of his faults of character, which were plain enough last night, he is a man who may make his mark, not that my love for him depends on that. But I am no longer in love with him. And every detail in our lives is being poisoned by this uncertainty and agitation.'

'If that is really so, the sooner you tell him the better for us all . . . but there's one thing I want to say . . . at least I don't want to say it, but I have been meaning to say it for several days and I must. . . . If you find, when you see him, that after all you *are* in love and you both want to go away together . . . I am willing to help you to arrange it. I can very easily say that I have to see D'Argenson in Paris, and suggest taking you with me for a week. We'll take your car and when we arrive at Boulogne you can go off with Carlo wherever you like. Don't worry about money . . .'

'You are extraordinary,' said Venetia.

'You keep on saying that, but it's not true. I would strangle Carlo, if I could do it without being found out. But that does not prevent me from trying to see it all through your eyes. It's not easy. I keep telling myself that you have changed. It's so hard for me to believe and understand—because I haven't.'

'I don't think that I have changed as much as you think I have.'

'But . . . then, why? How did it come about?'

'My life has been empty. You spend your life thinking about jets, or wind-tunnels, or fatigue in metals. I don't know or care what the words mean. I can't help you. I can't alter you. I can't interest you. It seemed possible to try and create someone out of Carlo; to educate a brilliant young man—he has plenty of intelligence—I might have been able to give him the chance to learn to think, and to feel, and to speak: to distinguish values. . . . It seemed to give my life a purpose.'

'Sebastian . . .'

'Whatever happens, Sebastian will be himself. Although he is only seventeen his feet are planted firmly on the ground. Compared with him, Carlo is all at sea. Sebastian will never owe anything important to me any more. Just like you.'

'But I am dependent on you. I suppose I oughtn't to say that, because you are not in love with me.'

'Perhaps I am not. But I love you more than I thought I did, Toby.'

'If I could only believe that. But I don't believe you any more . . .

Venetia stopped Toby's mouth with a kiss.

They said no more, and soon after breakfast she rang up Carlo's hotel, and then drove off. Directly Angela heard the sound of the car, she ran to the window and, catching sight of a flash of red, dressed and went downstairs. There was a dried-up kipper and some cold coffee. She swallowed them and felt that the avenging angel would be strong enough to carry out its mission.

Meanwhile Toby had gone into his study and locked the door. He felt that he could not go on: that the task he had set himself was beyond his capacity for endurance. Now that Venetia was perhaps on the point of breaking with Carlo, a sour spitefulness had taken possession of him which might drive her to reverse her decision. It was as though the sight of Carlo at the party had made her repellent as well as him. He could not believe in her making a final break. She could not have gone to see Carlo that morning without wishing and expecting him to make love to her. Yet she was also sincerely imagining that she would make a final break with him. The two things seemed to Toby to be in complete contradiction. If a woman breaks off a love affair, it is because she no longer wants to go to bed: if she still wants to see her lover, she will find plenty of excuses for one last time after another last time. The sense of power which her affair with Carlo had given her, the pleasure of torturing which was still almost entirely unconscious, was something that she would not voluntarily give up. But a break there must be. He would not continue to share his wife with that insolent, oily creature. If she came back without having broken with Carlo permanently, she would find that she had driven him at last to take the initiative. Toby began to write.

DEAREST VENETIA,

If, as I expect, you have found it too painful to break finally with C. M., I have decided that we must separate. He made it plain last night that this is his wish also. I have done my best to see things through your eyes, and to be reasonable. The more I think about it, the less reason does there seem why you should continue to live with me. Our relationship is almost entirely one-sided. It is not as though we had children to consider—for at sixteen Sebastian is practically grown up. I shall tell him the facts, and he can make his own plans. I shall probably go out to India this winter.

Fortunately I have enough money at present for us to be able to part without too much change in our scale of living. I suggest paying you £800 a year free of tax, paid quarterly and without conditions—I mean irrespective of whom you choose to live with. With your own money this should be enough to keep you comfortable. I cannot guarantee keeping this up, as my income depends upon my earnings, but I will do my best.

I can see that this reads like a cold letter. I don't feel cold—only I cannot go on.

Yours, TOBY

With the letter in his pocket, Toby felt armed for whatever might happen. But, having made his decision, he felt no calmer. While he was writing, his pen had trembled so violently that he needed all his will-power to write legibly. Wondering if his shaking were partly due to a hangover from the previous night, he opened a left-over bottle of champagne, drank three glasses and felt slightly revived.

Suppose, Toby asked himself, that Venetia came back saying that she had finally broken off her affair, what would the future hold then? What would they each have learned from the experience? And how could he make her sufficiently happy to prevent another man taking Carlo's place? What she had said that morning was true—not the whole of the truth, but a good part of it. Henceforward he must put Venetia before his work: not only her comfort, but her amusement must come first. Taking a flat in London, where Venetia and he could live, instead of spending his time in the club and leaving her in the country, would be one obvious change.

Perhaps Angela was a more poisonous influence than he guessed. Sebastian could not endure her; she had been getting a good deal on his own nerves; why should Venetia alone not dislike her constantly being with them? Then both Venetia and Sebastian loved boats, and were good at everything connected with water. Why not spend the summer holidays cruising in a five- or ten-ton ketch? Get away altogether, and make their first landfall at Flores in the Azores?

Then perhaps what she had once said about getting mouldy at The Old Forge meant that she would like to get away from Wiltshire altogether. Well—if she felt like that, why not? They were free.

Asking himself these questions revived Toby even more than the champagne had done. If, by any chance, Carlo had tipped the scales against himself by that performance last night, then the future held a gleam of hope.

'I'm sorry about last night,' said Carlo, after he had got into the car and Venetia was driving out of Newbury. 'Your'—Carlo wanted to say *Toby* or *husband*, but found that he could not use either word —'your lame duck put one over me and I couldn't take it. . . . I wanted to tell you, so that you should understand. Anyway the bloody party is over. . . .'

He did not speak again until Venetia had driven off the road and stopped the car in an oak wood.

'I didn't sleep last night because I had to get

133

everything clear,' said Carlo, 'and it's just this: Are you game enough to come away with me now?'

Venetia shook her head and began to speak, but Carlo would not listen and went on:

'You can see better than I can that I've a long way to go before I get into his income bracket. But I shall. I've got big ideas. . . . If you have the guts to start again with me low down the ladder . . .'

'My dear . . . my dear Carlo. Please understand . . . please believe . . . it doesn't matter to me whether you make money, or sweep out the sawdust in the ring. Money doesn't come into it. But I've come to say good-bye, and that we mustn't see one another again.'

'You want to break off because you think I'm not a good risk? That's it, is it?' Carlo asked angrily, but Venetia's expression was so blank that he continued:

'You wouldn't back me to win, or even for a place, if your lame duck is a runner?'

'I'm quite sure you will be a bigger success, and make more money than Toby has done. You want it more than he does. . . . He really only goes on because he wants perfection in aircraft engineering, and he has become a sort of mascot to the young designers . . .'

'If you love me and think I have a future, what more do you want?' asked Carlo.

'I do love you. But I only love you in the same

way that I love Toby.   I'm not *in* love with you, and I thought I was.'

'You're saying you made a mistake?'

'I was unhappy.   I thought life was empty.   I can't explain what a lot your love and the excitement of your love has done for me.   I can't ever thank you enough.   I have no regrets.'

'A pretty parting scene,' sneered Carlo.

'If I went with you now, I shouldn't stay with you.'

'I wouldn't easily let you go.'

'Loving you seemed somehow a proof of my freedom.   If I were to live with you, you would take my freedom away.'

'You mean you won't ever be faithful to one man?'

'That isn't at all what I meant, though I suppose it may be true.   I don't feel like ever having another love affair in my life.'

Carlo looked at Venetia with an odd smile.

'A dame like you has got to belong to some man. You know that your lame duck won't put up a fight to keep you and that I would.   That's what scares you.'

Venetia's whole expression had changed.   She shook her head, and Carlo saw that one or two tears that were running down her cheeks were diverted from their course.   But she somehow managed to avoid bursting into tears, and to control her voice, though she spoke in little more than a whisper.

'Do stop talking like a bad film. . . . You take

for granted too much that all my motives are selfish: first that I want money and security, then that I can't make any sacrifice for anyone. You really think I am a bitch and nothing but a bitch, and that is the complete explanation.'

'You claim to be one.'

Venetia shook her head, and again Carlo noticed a tear that was thrown out of its course and almost reached the point of her jaw.

'No, I don't. I'm breaking off with you because I should make both Sebastian and Toby desperately unhappy, and because I don't feel in the least certain that we should be happy, or even that I should be able to continue to live with you. It would be certain bad on one side and very uncertain good on the other.'

'Don't start preaching.'

It was a second or two before Venetia realized that he said this because she had used the words good and bad, which was instantaneously followed by the reflection that Carlo and she spoke such different languages that she could not hope to explain her motives, or her feelings. But why should she even try, since however successful she might be momentarily in getting him to understand, he would call her a bitch whenever he remembered her in the years to come?

Carlo, however, seemed almost to have been reading her thoughts when he said:

'I think it's true about your kid. He counts a hell of a lot more than the lame duck. I should have to look out for myself if he were a couple of years older.'

Venetia felt that she must somehow bring this unbearable conversation to an end.

'What does it matter what my reasons are? We have got to part, and we loved each other . . .'

But Carlo was not to be side-tracked.

'I bet if you sacrifice us to the kid you'll be doing him a real bad turn. You'll keep hold of him just at the age when he ought to get away from you. You talk about wanting freedom, but that's so much hot air for a woman. But it's life or death for a boy of sixteen. He'll never grow to be a man unless he gets away from you.'

Although Venetia had realized that it was useless to speak, and that the less Carlo and she said to one another before they parted the better, she could not resist saying:

'It is just because freedom isn't hot air to me that I shall make sure that Sebastian has every chance to get away.' Then suddenly changing her tone, she said: 'Oh, Carlo, why can't you believe that I'm doing what I honestly think best? It doesn't make it any better for you to think that I'm only selfish. You must know that I love you.' And she caught hold of one of his hands. In a moment she was clasped in a grip of iron, her head was pressed back, and she found herself lying on the thin grass and broken twigs, all white with pigeon droppings.

'It's a good thing that I'm an ambitious man or I might strangle you,' said Carlo six minutes later.

Then, as she was moving towards the car, he said:

'I'm not leaving until the afternoon train, in case you should change your mind.'

'Good-bye, Carlo,' said Venetia. The tears were pouring from her eyes, and it was damnably difficult to see well enough to drive the car. But she had to get away quickly . . . quickly . . . and for ever.

'You're not leaving me in this bloody wood,' shouted Carlo in sudden realization, as the car started moving, and he dashed forward, but the path was too narrow for him to pass, and though he just touched the handle of the door the little car suddenly accelerated and it was jerked away.

Carlo was walking down the road, still cursing her, when a taxi, which Venetia had sent out from Newbury, drew up beside him.

'Are you the gentleman that the lady sent me to take to the Rose and Crown?' the driver asked.

10

A NGELA was at the window watching, and saw
Venetia drive up, and then heard her go to her bedroom, and immediately afterwards the sound of
Toby clumping rapidly upstairs after her. She
slipped out of her bedroom and ran downstairs
silently to the telephone.

'It's all over,' said Venetia, as Toby went into
the room. 'That's all you want to know, isn't
it?'

'You mean with him—not with me?' he asked.

'With Carlo,' replied Venetia in an exhausted
voice. Toby's voice seemed to come from a long
way off, and she longed for him to go away. However he had sat down on the bed, and was breathing
heavily:

'Have you really broken it off with him? I felt
convinced you wouldn't, and that you would make
it up with him. I've spent the whole morning writing
a letter to tell you that we must separate. Well, I
can burn it now.'

Downstairs, in Toby's study, Angela was ringing
up the Rose and Crown. She asked for Carlo.

'The gentleman went out about two hours ago,

and has not yet returned,' said a woman's voice. That made it easier.

'I want to leave a message. Please tell him that I must see him to-night. That it is most important, but that I am going out now and shall not be back until half-past eleven. Tell him I shall leave the front door unbolted, and that he is to come in. Yes, that's all.' Angela rang off. Five minutes later, there was a ring, and Angela, who had stayed in the study, answered the call. It was Carlo.

'Mr. Barnard's secretary speaking . . . I am afraid that you have just missed her. They all went off, three or four minutes ago, and they won't be back till late to-night. . . . No, I don't know where they've gone. Actually Mrs. Barnard seemed to have forgotten all about it, and was rather late in getting off. . . . Would you like me to leave a note to say that you rang up? You see, I shall have gone to bed before they get back. . . . Good-bye.' Angela rang off hurriedly as she heard Toby open the door. He was carrying a hot-water bottle.

'What was that, Angela?' he asked.

'Some reporter trying to get hold of you about last night's party. I think it was a Sunday paper. I told him you would be out all day.'

'What a wonderful watchdog you are! Have you seen the tube of codeine anywhere? Venetia's gone to bed. You might tell Mrs. Ball she won't be down for lunch, and doesn't want to be disturbed.'

'The effects of the party, I suppose,' said Angela. 'The codeine is on the top shelf in the dining-room cupboard.'

Toby went off and Angela's expression changed to one of fury.

'She must have been copulating with that awful man in the middle of the morning,' she said to herself, and shuddered with disgust. 'Well, it ought to open Toby's eyes when Mr. Carlo comes bursting into the house in the small hours.'

The more Sebastian thought about Carlo Marx, the more convinced he was that his first suspicions were correct. Carlo had clearly been a fish out of water at the party, and why should he have come to it at all? The ulterior motive, which stuck out a mile, was to get an idea of the lay-out of the house, in order to burgle it afterwards. Sebastian would have liked to have questioned his mother, but she had gone to bed and was not to be disturbed. He did not want to tackle his father, who would laugh at his suspicions. So Sebastian sought out Angela, who was typing the shorthand notes she had made from Toby's dictation the previous morning.

'About this chap who calls himself Karl Marx . . .' he began. At his words Angela's mouth dropped open, and she blushed violently. Sebastian broke off and stared at her in surprise. It was a moment or two before she pulled herself together, and said:

'Well, what about him?'

'He's a Communist agent,' said Sebastian.

'Whatever makes you think that?'

'His name for one thing.'

Angela gave a hysterical giggle.

'His name is Carlo, not Karl with a K.'

'What does it matter how you spell it? Don't you see it is a marvellous double bluff? Nobody would suspect a man who called himself Karl, or Carlo, Marx of being a Communist. That is the perfect double bluff, and the single bluff is coming to the party in a white tie and tails.'

'Does it matter if he is a Communist?'

'I believe he's coming back to steal what's in there . . .' and Sebastian pointed to the big safe, which stood in a corner of the room. 'I think he may burgle the house to-night.'

'Don't be such an idiot,' exclaimed Angela. 'Carlo is a friend of your mother's. He knows nothing about Toby, or his work, and there are no papers in that safe which could interest him, even if he were a Russian agent with snow on his boots. Toby is only concerned with civil aircraft. Try and be your age and think up something better, if you want to fancy you are living in a thriller. Buzz off and let me get on with my work.'

Angela's vehemence and ridicule would have over-whelmed Sebastian had Toby not told him about the top secret plans. Either they were so secret that she knew nothing about them, or else she was lying. But he thought it better not to insist further.

'Keep your hair on, Angela. But I thought the name was clever.'

'Don't tell Toby, you half-wit, or you'll never hear the last of it,' said Angela.

Sebastian went away convinced in his suspicions of Carlo, and filled with new suspicions that Angela was in league with him. She had completely given herself away, blushing and being upset like that, and then denying that there were secret papers in the safe! Probably Carlo had been her lover and was blackmailing her. . . . Obviously she had told him that Carlo was an admirer of his mother's to put him off the scent.

And suddenly it struck him that in his practical joke on Toby he had hit the nail on the head. Angela had Communist affiliations! Was it not the irony of life that his invention should turn out to be the sober truth—and that as a result, it would be more difficult than ever to persuade Toby of it? It would be useless to warn him: he must handle it himself.

Sebastian's visit alarmed Angela, and she suddenly regretted her precipitate plot to decoy Carlo into the house at midnight. It occurred to her that he might be dangerous; he might attack Toby who, with his crippled leg, would be no match for the younger man. If Toby were injured she would never, never forgive herself. In any case it was probable that the plot would be traced to her.

'That doesn't really matter,' she said aloud. 'It doesn't really matter even if Toby never forgives me,' and Angela swallowed down her tears.

'Only one thing matters now: that he should be saved from that foul, treacherous, lying woman! How can anyone be so horrible? I don't mind her being cruel to me—but she is so confident in her wickedness, so absolutely shameless, steeped in sin. Evil. Oh, Toby! Toby! Toby! I can't live without you. But I would rather do that than endure to see you so ill-used any longer. If Venetia tries to wriggle out of being caught with Carlo to-night, I shall accuse her in front of Toby and give him the proofs of her adultery.'

Angela unlocked her trunk and took out the collection which she had started with the counterfoils of the Swindon *Palais de Danse*. There were two letters from Carlo which she had stolen from Venetia's writing-desk, a hotel bill which she had found crumpled up in her handbag, and a copy of the hotel register from Swindon which she had visited on purpose to obtain it. Angela read the collection for the twentieth time. She would hand these damning papers to Toby.

'So long as I free him to lead a clean and honourable life, I don't mind. I'll sacrifice myself. It's my duty.'

Venetia did not come down to supper, but even so it was an embarrassing meal.

'I'm going to turn in early and advise both of you to do the same,' said Toby, putting the tray, which he had brought down from the bedroom, on the table.

'I certainly shall,' said Sebastian. 'I'm more than half asleep.'

'I shall sit up for a bit. I'll lock up if you like,' said Angela.

Toby went upstairs again with a hot-water bottle, and to Angela's relief Sebastian did not linger. She thought it was lucky she had scotched his idea of a burglary.

At a quarter to twelve, Angela turned out the lights in the house, eased the front door open and went out to watch in the garden. The night was warm and full of the scent of hay and of night-flowering stocks. Pale stars studded the sky: the moon would be rising in another half-hour and there was light all round the eastern and northern horizon. Angela felt confident and happy. She was going to frame that foul creature.

'Let justice be done though the heavens fall! Which means though I lose my job!' she exclaimed, looking up at the pale stars. Just as the moon rose, the lights of a car came flickering up the chalk lane. It stopped by the old chalk pit, and Angela could see that it was being turned round. Then the headlights were switched off. Angela at once walked back to the house, switched on the hall light and went upstairs. Her heart was beating, as she knocked on the bedroom door. There was no response and no time to lose. She knocked again, opened the door and put her head in.

'Hullo, what's the matter?' asked Toby.

'It's Angela. I want to speak to Venetia for a moment.'

'What is it?' she repeated yawning, and coming to the doorway. Her long black hair hung down over one shoulder to below her breast, and her nylon night-gown was transparent. She blinked, half-asleep, while Angela beckoned to her from across the landing.

'Carlo Marx is downstairs. He says he must speak to you. It's something very urgent.'

Venetia stared at her in round-eyed wonder.

'Carlo? Tell him to wait a moment. I'll get my dressing-gown.' She went back into the bedroom and shut the door, leaving Angela infuriated by her apparent calm.

'Toby darling,' said Venetia. 'Angela has just told me that Carlo is downstairs. Do you think he has gone mad? I suppose I must go and see him.'

'Perhaps it would be better if I spoke to him, and found out what he wants. I'll tell him that you've asked me to tell him to go away: that you don't want to see him again, and that in any case he is not to turn up in the middle of the night.'

'Perhaps that is the best thing: you'll be able to keep your temper.'

'I suppose it isn't some accident?' asked Toby.

'He told me he was catching the afternoon train,' replied Venetia. 'Perhaps he wants to kill me. I wonder if it's safe for you?'

Toby fastened on his artificial leg without bothering to conceal the operation from Venetia, and, watching, she felt a new tenderness for him. Then Toby put on his dressing-gown.

All this took a little time, and when he reached the landing he could hear voices.

'I came here because of a telephone message, by appointment. I spoke to your father's secretary, and she told me your parents were out all day and would only get back late,' Carlo was saying in a curious tone of voice. There was a tremendous draught.

When Toby got half-way down the stairs, he saw that Sebastian was standing in the open hall door with a double-barrelled gun levelled at Carlo, who was holding his hands in the air. His complexion was green.

'I've caught him. He's a Communist come to burgle your safe,' cried Sebastian as he saw his father.

'Put that gun down, Sebastian.'

'I bet he's got a pistol in his pocket.'

'Put it down and shut the door and go up to bed. It's not what you think it is.'

'You don't know half,' replied Sebastian, lowering the muzzle of the gun. 'Angela is in league with him. I saw her go out and wait for him in the garden. When she came back she left the front door un-latched. I was waiting outside for him.'

'That's very interesting. But shut the door and cut along. Mr. Marx and I want to have a few words in private.'

'I'll stay in the hall with the gun, in case I'm wanted,' said Sebastian.

Carlo had said nothing, but he went into the dining-room with alacrity when Toby opened the door.

'I must apologize for my son. I had pulled his leg about secret papers, and he naturally thought you were a burglar.'

'You may think it clever to frame me and try to frighten me with a gun, but you won't get anywhere,' said Carlo.

'Sit down and have a glass of brandy—or whisky if you prefer it—and just tell me why you are here.'

Carlo accepted the whisky and drank off the glass. Then in a rather truculent tone, he asked:

'So you deny having decoyed me here?'

'Neither I nor Venetia had the slightest desire to see you, either here, or anywhere else.'

'I would prefer to hear that from her own lips, old man.'

'She was fast asleep when Angela woke us both up, and said you were in the hall asking to see Venetia.'

'You say that your secretary said that I had asked to see her?'

'Yes, she woke us up to tell us so.'

'I had only just stepped into the hall when your son told me to put my hands up, or he would blow my guts out. I never saw your secretary or spoke to her—except on the telephone this afternoon.'

'But why did you come here?'

'I can't tell you that, until I've seen your wife.'

'Have another glass of whisky,' said Toby, pouring it out. 'You talk about being decoyed here. But since neither I nor Venetia, nor Sebastian decoyed you, it must have been Angela. She seems to have known you were coming. Nobody else did.'

'Sez you.'

Toby got up and limped into the hall. Sebastian was sitting on the stairs, with the gun on his knees.

'Give me that gun, will you? And go and ask your mother to come down for a minute.'

Toby took the gun, extracted the cartridges, put them in his pocket, and stood it in the corner of the hall. Then he went back into the dining-room and shut the door. Neither Carlo nor he spoke until the door was opened, and Venetia came in. She looked with cold dislike and contempt at each of the two men.

'Venetia, did you ever ask Carlo to come here to-night?'

'My God, no!'

She had scarcely spoken when the door was suddenly thrown open and Angela appeared standing in it.

'Don't listen to her, Toby. Don't let her lie her way out of it. She has been deceiving you all the summer with that man there. I have proof and I won't let them deceive you any longer.'

'Are you responsible for Mr. Marx coming here to-night?' asked Toby.

'Yes. But for a good reason. I knew they were deceiving you and I wanted you to catch them together.'

'That's enough, Angela. Will you please go up to your room?'

'But you must believe me . . . I have all the facts you'll need when you divorce her . . . when and where she stayed with him . . . copies from hotel registers . . . photographs of some of his letters which prove adultery . . . you can't be blind to it any longer . . .'

'Toby has known all about my relations with Carlo for months,' said Venetia. 'You have tried to make mischief; have turned yourself into a detective, spying on things that have nothing to do with you,

150

and have only made a nuisance of yourself in the middle of the night.'

For a moment Angela stood her ground. Then she caught Toby's eye and turned to leave the room, but Sebastian suddenly blocked the doorway. He was carrying the gun again, and from his first words it was clear that he had been listening.

'So Angela has been shown up at last. Thank God for that,' he said quietly.

Angela started back angrily as though she were afraid of him.

'You silly, melodramatic boy playing at Communist burglars! Am I "shown up" because your father is dishonoured, and your mother is a loose woman?' she said acidly.

There was a long silence. At one moment Venetia made as though to speak, but Toby silenced her with a gesture.

'Yes, Angela,' said Sebastian. 'You are revealed as a scheming crazy creature. Thanks to you I have found out that Karl Marx is my mother's lover, and not a Communist or a burglar. So what? Answer that? What business is that of yours?'

Once again there was a silence. Then Sebastian turned to look at Toby and Venetia, and said slowly:

'What business is it of mine either? But you think you have a right to judge them, Angela,' he said with sudden rage. 'My father without honour . . . and my mother a . . . Get out of here, you hell-cat.' He made a sudden motion with his gun for her to leave the room, and without a word she scuttled past him. Sebastian took a moment or two to regain his self-control and then turned to Carlo.

'So you thought I had decoyed you here and was threatening to shoot you out of jealousy, or family pride, or revenge?'

'Something like that, sonny.'

Sebastian looked at Carlo and said slowly: 'I would have shot you just now if I had known . . . but any man would be her lover if he had the chance . . . I thought it would be grand to get the gun and ambush you . . . but it wasn't needed . . .'

'You said you were through with me this morning,' said Carlo, suddenly addressing Venetia as though Sebastian and Toby did not exist, 'and it looked like it was the finish. I never thought of coming here . . . or of your kid finding out. But now he does know, what's holding you? Come away with me right now. I'm sorry about what I did in the wood. I am really. But you know I'm alive. I'm not a plaster saint like old duck-foot—and I'm not acting in a Western like the kid. I'd give you a real life and you'll get clear of this lot. Take a chance on it.'

Toby and Sebastian had turned to look at Venetia as Carlo was speaking and saw her expression, which had been one of haughty disgust, become transformed by his words until a grave smile lit up her face with tenderness. She shook her head slightly, and when she spoke it was in a low voice.

'It is like you, Carlo, to have said that and to have given me another chance. I know you would give me everything that you could according to your ideas. I believe that I thought that I was free to choose. But I'm not. You and I have not got enough in common. I shall never leave Toby.'

Carlo stood up, his sallow face had flushed dark with anger, and he took an uncertain step towards the door.

'It's damned late. Can I run you back to your hotel?' asked Toby suddenly.

'God rot you! So you've found your voice at last!' exclaimed Carlo. And then, suddenly changing his tone to one of mock gentility, he added: 'Thank you very much—but I hired a car and it's waiting down the road.' And then, in sudden rage, he repeated: 'God rot you!'

Toby did not speak, and as though conscious that something further was required, Carlo muttered: 'Good night and good-bye!' and walked out of the room, through the hall into the night.

Sebastian made a sudden gesture, and bowing his head because he had suddenly discovered that he could not say good night to his mother, hurried after him out of the room, shutting the door behind him. He had been a participant in his parents' world, he had played his part in their drama, and now he felt suddenly that he was an intruder in it. He had no judgements to make: he could not criticize or condemn. He was aware that he knew nothing. He was not sure any longer of his love for them.

When Venetia and Toby followed, they found the hall door still open, and going out for a few moments into the garden, looked at the newly risen moon and drew in deep breaths of the perfumes of the night. After observing that the pale stars were still fixed in their constellations, they went back to bed.

THE END